The Widow

&

The War Correspondent

By Linda Shenton Matchett

Chapter One

Journalist Cora Strealer winced, gripping her pencil and notepad tighter as the burly man next to her tromped on her toes and cheered with the rest of the crowd. Whistles and applause filled the high school gymnasium, reverberating off the wood floor and cement walls. The largest room in her small town overflowed with members of the press, the public, and leaders of their tiny municipality anticipating the appearance of Rita Hayworth at the war bond rally. Someone had tried to purge the decades-old smell of sweaty teenage basketball players, but the acrid stink of perspiration clung to the crisp scent of bleach.

The last two rallies had been well-attended, but the announcement about the beautiful movie star's presence brought folks from miles around, including newspapermen from Boston, who wouldn't normally give their event a second glance. She rolled her eyes. The only reason she'd gotten the assignment instead of Oscar Blanding, the other full-time writer for their weekly paper, was his hospitalization. Much to his chagrin, he'd developed appendicitis and required surgery to remove the offending organ. Bad for him, fantastic for her.

Would this be the big break she was waiting for?

She sighed. Probably not. As soon as he was released, Oscar would be back to writing the major news, and she'd be relegated to fluff pieces: graduations, engagement parties, retirement parties, and weddings with the occasional selectmen's meeting thrown in for good measure.

Her writing was strong. Mr. Paxton, her editor, admitted that pearl several months ago during yet another argument as to why she wasn't allowed to cover feature stories. Maybe she could weasel her way into an interview with Miss Hayworth, then Mr. Paxton would have to let her do the article. Once it was published, the Associated Press or United Press could pick it up, sending it around the globe in one of the big newspapers. Then she'd get real coverage, a shot at the big leagues.

The jubilant man knocked into her again, this time sending Doris crashing into the wall. She gritted her teeth and craned her neck to search for another spot from which to cover the event. Surely, there was a place she could stand and see everything without getting engulfed in the mass of humanity.

Sunlight glinted through the windows overhead. Doris squinted, and her gaze caught movement near the bleachers on the far side of the room. Perfect. Unless every other journalist in the room thought of hiding out underneath the wooden seating, she'd have a decent view without the chaos.

Fortunately, the benches weren't made of metal or the scrap collection committee would have snatched them along with the railings, cook pots, and other items that had disappeared over the course of the war.

She flattened her body against the wall and squeezed past the revelers. What would they be like when Miss Hayworth greeted them?

"Excuse me. Sorry. Coming through." Doris threaded her way along the perimeter of the room. She tried to ignore the frowns and glares from the attendees. Weren't they happy there was one less person in front of them?

Fifteen minutes of pushing and slithering brought her to the bleachers. She surveyed the undulating mass of people then ducked underneath the stands.

"Cora. I wondered when you'd come to your senses and join me." Her friend since elementary school, Amanda Norton, stood under the bleachers, a mischievous grin on her face. Ebony hair swept up into a smooth chignon, and wearing a cobalt-blue blouse with a black pencil skirt and stiletto heels, she looked every inch the executive she was.

"You look fabulous as always. Did you come straight from work?"

"Yeah, Dad said one of the family should represent us, and he had a bunch of phone calls to make."

"I still can't believe he gave you the manufacturing director's position over your brother." Cora pushed down tendrils of jealousy. What would it be like to have a challenging job and be taken seriously?

"Phil didn't want the job. He's happy tinkering in Research and Development." Amanda shrugged. "The board of directors was the difficult mountain to climb, but Dad convinced them I'm the best person. I think they're waiting for me to fail." She shook her head. "Not going to happen. Anyway, enough about me. I don't wish the man ill will, but Oscar's appendicitis worked out for you, huh?"

"I'm hoping to score an interview with Miss Hayworth, but there are so many big-name reporters, I don't stand a chance."

Amanda smiled like a cat who'd finished a bowl of cream. "What if I were to tell you a certain movie star is going to tour our plant tomorrow, and I could get you time with her?"

Cora squealed. "You're the best. This might be my big break."

⸻ ⸱⸱⸱●◆●⸱⸱⸱ ⸻

Cora threw back the covers and jumped out of bed. The wooden floor was cold on her bare feet as she hurried to the closet to select her outfit. The smell of pancakes filtered from the kitchen. Moving back home after her husband was killed with so many others during the attack at Pearl Harbor, she slept in the bedroom that had been hers since childhood. Her gaze went to the framed photograph of Brian. After two-and-a-half years, his death still seemed unreal. Trapped in the USS *Arizona* when the ship went down, his body hadn't been returned.

No body. No casket. No viewing. When would she stop looking for him to come through the door?

She closed her eyes for a long moment searching her heart. Sure, she missed Brian, but with their whirlwind courtship and even shorter marriage, she hardly felt like a widow. Was she wrong to have those feelings? Her mother would be horrified.

Opening her eyes, Cora continued to run her hands over the clothes hanging in her closet. What did one wear when meeting a famous celebrity? Especially someone as elegant and refined as Miss Hayworth.

Her fingers fell on the sage-colored silk suit she'd worn for her wedding. Heart hammering, she pulled the outfit off its hanger and walked to the full-length mirror in the corner. She held the suit in front of her, studying her reflection in the glass. Blonde hair fell past her shoulders in a tangled mass, and her blue eyes picked up the green from the suit and seemed almost turquoise.

"Ugh. I look like a teenaged cheerleader with these freckles. No one would guess I'm thirty-one years old." Rubbing her eyes that burned from lack of sleep, she yawned. How many times had she awakened with another idea for the interview? She glanced at the illegible scrawl on the top sheet of her notebook.

Time was wasting. She hurried to the bathroom and fifteen minutes later was dressed, ready to go. She stuffed the steno pad and extra pencils into her pocketbook and skipped down the stairs.

A car horn beeped outside, and she opened the door to wave at Amanda. Racing into the kitchen, she kissed her mother on the cheek and grabbed a piping hot pancake. Rolling it up, she blew on the hot cake before taking a bite. She snatched a napkin from the table. "Yummy as always, Mom. See you later."

"Have fun, honey."

"Thanks." Cora bit off another piece of the pancake as she left the house and rushed to Amanda's car. Considered an essential war worker, she was assigned a C gasoline ration sticker, giving her more than the usual four gallons per week that most people were allotted.

Nearly out of her own rationed amount of fuel, Cora was thrilled when Amanda offered to pick her up. Bicycling to the plant in her suit hardly seemed like an option. She wiped her fingers on the napkin then opened the door and climbed inside the back seat of the car. Her jaw dropped, and her breath quickened.

Seated beside her, Miss Hayworth smiled and held out her hand. "Mrs. Strealer? A pleasure to meet you."

Cora's heart threatened to jump from her chest, and she took a deep breath as she shook the movie star's hand. "Uh, actually I use my maiden name for my byline, but you can call me Cora."

"Perfect, and please call me Rita. We don't need formalities with just us girls here." She smoothed the skirt on her emerald-green dress then straightened the pillbox hat set on her gleaming titian-colored hair, orange highlights glinting in the early morning sun. Her smile was genuine as she patted Cora's knee. "How long have you been a newspaperwoman?"

"Since high school. I got my degree in English then moved to Hawaii when my husband was assigned there. I wrote for the *Honolulu Star Advertiser*, but after he was killed, I moved back home, and now I write for the local paper."

"I'm sorry to hear about your husband."

Cora shrugged. "It was a long time ago."

From the driver's seat, Amanda gestured over her shoulder. "Cora's a great writer. I think she should apply to become a war correspondent. Especially with her experience at Pearl."

Face heating, Cora shook her head. "Amanda, Miss Hayworth…Rita…doesn't want to hear about my life."

"On the contrary." Rita smiled. "It will be nice to focus on someone other than myself. I appreciate what my celebrity status can do for the boys in the service and the country's morale, but being the center of attention is fatiguing. Tell me about the opportunity."

Licking her lips, Cora gulped. "In order to be a war correspondent overseas, I need to receive accreditation from the government which involves a lengthy background check and a physical. Working for such a tiny newspaper, I'm not sure I'll pass."

"How about the Associated Press or United Press?" Rita cocked her head.

"Don't they have plenty of staff already?"

"This war spans the globe. There can never be too many reporters. I'll write you a letter of introduction to the London bureau chief for the UP. Will that help?"

Cora's eyes widened. "Well…uh—"

Amanda clapped her hands. "You're a peach, Rita. A recommendation from you should get our girl in."

"I'm happy to help. We gals need to stick together."

"Thank you, Miss—Rita. I appreciate the offer. I haven't decided to pursue going overseas."

"You can't let this pass you by, Cora. You're stagnating here in this one-horse town. Nothing is keeping you here. Certainly not this newspaper that doesn't appreciate your talent. I say you go for it. Don't you agree, Rita?"

Rita turned to Cora. "What do you want? Are you happy with your current position? You need to make the decision that's right for you, but I will say that if I hadn't made some changes in my life, I wouldn't be the star I am today. Sometimes shaking things up is good. Perhaps being a war correspondent will be the best thing to happen to you. Maybe not, but you won't know unless you try."

Cora slumped against the seat. "You're right. I'm stuck in a rut. Here in town, everyone feels sorry for me. They tiptoe around, afraid to talk about the war or my husband. A fresh start where no one knows about Brian might be just the ticket." Grinning, she straightened and crossed her arms. "Look out, world. Here I come."

Chapter Two

Van Toppel hunched over the cantankerous Smith Corona and banged out his latest newspaper article. He coughed and waved one hand to dispel the fetid cigarette smoke that wafted past his face. Turning, he glared at Harry Bronson who sat at the next typewriter. "Hey, blow that foul smog in the other direction. Some of us in here are trying to breathe."

"Sorry, farmboy. It's the only vice my wife will let me have." Harry smirked and moved the ashtray filled with dozens of sooty butts to the far side of his machine. "You must hate London with the ever-present smell of coal. How'd you end up here?"

"Just lucky, I guess. How about you?"

"I put in for this gig. I'm hoping to get behind the scenes in North Africa or somewhere exotic like Italy or Egypt, but I gotta do my time in this fair city first." He stubbed out the cigarette and poked at the typewriter keys. "This war's gonna be over soon, and I want to make sure I get some hot bylines. Get a chance at a Pulitzer, you know?"

"Yeah, I know." Van sighed and read what he'd written. Not bad. A couple of editing tweaks, and it would be ready to go to the censor, an annoying reality of a reporter's life in wartime. If he was lucky, the guy wouldn't change a word, but more than likely he'd remove a bit to prove his worth. Van had learned what was acceptable the hard way: through trial and error with more than a few articles scrapped in their entirety.

He added a few more sentences, yanked the page from the roller, then performed a quick edit. Done. Rising, he slung his sport coat over his shoulder and threaded his way through the rows of tables that held dozens of typewriters in Broadcasting House's third floor room assigned to the print journalists.

Completed fourteen years ago, the Art Deco building took four years to construct, with three of its twelve floors underground. The BBC graciously set aside room for the reporters who'd swarmed the city at the onset of the war. Being able to borrow a machine meant he didn't have to tote a portable. A benefit for someone who had traveled from the northern tip in Scotland to the southern coast overlooking the Channel.

Shrugging his arms into his coat, he headed down the stairs to the lobby where he dropped off his article in the pouch destined for the Ministry of Information offices where the censors were housed. Time to clear his head and scrounge up some more news.

He pushed open the door and walked outside, grit crunching underfoot. Squinting in the midday sunshine, he shielded his eyes and surveyed the pedestrians who scurried past, intent on their destinations. Puffy cotton-ball clouds scudded overhead in the robin's-egg-blue sky. A bus stopped in front of the building, emitting fumes and passengers before thundering away. He wrinkled his nose against the stench: nothing like the pure, clean air in Iowa where he'd been raised.

"Hey, Van. How goes the battle?" Gary Weymouth, a correspondent for Colliers, waved as he approached. "Did you already submit your piece?"

"Yeah, I'm going to prowl the city, see what I can come up with for another story. You?"

"Got a juicy one from Battersea Park. According to the detective sergeant on the scene, a young woman was found dead, and it appears to be murder."

Van frowned. "Murder in a time of war. Isn't there enough killing to go around?"

"I guess not." Gary leaned close. "Did you hear the other news, about the female correspondents they're going to saddle us with?"

"No, but it was bound to happen sooner or later. There are lots of lady reporters overseas. Why shouldn't they borrow the space? Margaret Bourke-White has been with *Life* for almost ten years now, and she covered the Blitz. I'm surprised we haven't seen her before now."

"Yeah, but I don't understand why they want to be here. To cover war."

"Because they're intelligent and curious. Like we are."

"They shouldn't be here. This is a man's job."

"You need to shed that Victorian attitude, Gary. Life as we know it is over. Gals have proven themselves capable to do any job set before them."

"Maybe, but I don't have to like it."

Another bus chugged past, a swirling black fog of exhaust in its wake. Van put his hand over his nose trying not to gag. He needed to get out of the city. The constant press of people and toxic smells were going to be the death of him.

Gary clapped him on the back. "Too bad the war couldn't happen somewhere nice and clean, eh?"

Van moved his hand and frowned. "London's streets were clean before the Jerries arrived with their bombs and incendiaries. Why is man so intent on destroying himself?"

"That's what we're here to find out." Gary waved his notebook. "Nice jawing with you, but I've got a story to write."

"Good luck with it. And try to be polite if any of those lady reporters show up."

"Sure. Just for you." Gary slipped through the crowd and into the building.

Stuffing his hands into his pockets, Van crossed the street then descended into the Tube station. Being below ground was nearly as bad as navigating the city streets. Teeming with people, the platform was dark with grime. How did the submariners spend months trapped in their metal cylinders?

Trapped. He snapped his fingers. England was littered with prisoner-of-war camps. Would the public be interested in how the POWs were housed and treated, many of whom were used in agricultural and nondefense work? Scoring interviews with the Germans would put faces on the enemy for his readers. Was that good or bad?

He whipped out his notebook and began to scribble ideas for slants on the article. Bumped from behind, his pencil skittered across the page, leaving a slash. He frowned and whirled to find the offender. A trio of women chattering like magpies stood nearby. Their laughter punctuated the buzz of conversation. Young and giggly, they seemed oblivious to anyone's presence but their own.

Were women like Bourke-White, Dickey Chapelle, Toni Frissell, and Hemingway's wife, Martha Gellhorn, the exception rather than the rule? Or did he believe his own rhetoric that women could do any job as well as a man? He had to admire their gumption, but was Gary right that they didn't belong over here?

With a shrug, he turned his attention back to his notebook. Philosophical considerations about women in the workplace were for another day. He had a story to ferret out.

Chapter Three

Cora clutched her pocketbook and followed the horde of journalists into London's Palace Theatre. More than three months had passed since she decided to take Miss Hayworth's advice and apply to become a war correspondent. The accreditation process had been lengthy and not without a few bumps, but a week ago she'd received her acceptance notice. Would the delay have been longer without the actress's letter of reference? Two days later, she was on an airplane to England. Her heart remained in her throat during most of the flight, but she refused to let the mostly male-occupied aircraft see her nervousness.

With a smile, she clutched her identification card, ready to flash it at one of the guards guiding the crowd into the auditorium. She was a full-fledged reporter with United Press and would show them they'd made the right decision by hiring her.

Bulldozed on all sides by cigarette- and cigar-smoking men, she tried to breathe through her mouth while attempting to hold her ground. She would not be relegated to the back row. The pungent, gray fog swirled above her head, and she swallowed a cough.

She reached the doorway to the amphitheater, held up her badge, and squeezed into the hall already half filled. Conversation and laughter blended into a cacophony of noise that bounced off the carved wood paneling and gleaming wood floors. Tucking her elbows to her sides and straightening to her full five-foot-three-inch height, she frowned. A head shorter than most of the attendees, she found herself staring at shoulders and backs. If Dickey Chapelle could climb the ranks from her diminutive size, so could she.

"Excuse me. Coming through, please." Cora pushed her way through the sea of people, voice more confident than she felt. "Make way. Thank you." As each man turned to see who was speaking, she slipped forward. Within minutes, she stood near the front of the room, where a single vacant seat beckoned from the middle of the third row. Without a second thought, she made a beeline for the chair, flanked on either side by middle-aged, Brylcreem-haired men in gray suits. A dollar said they would not be happy to see her.

Tightening her grip on her handbag, she stepped into the row and marched to the vacant seat. She flopped down with a sigh, smoothed her skirt, and ensured her blue cloche hat was still firmly pinned into place.

The man to her right scowled. "This is for reporters only, honey. You can't be here."

She gave him her brightest smile and dug out her ID card. "I am a reporter, *honey*, but thank you for clarifying that I'm in the right place." She held out her hand. "Cora Strealer, United Press."

His eyebrows shot up and disappeared into his hairline. Scowl deepening, he squinted at her badge then shook his head. "Didn't know they were letting more dames into the ranks. Well, keep your mouth shut and your eyes open, so you can see how the job should be done."

"Sir, I appreciate your advice, but I have no doubt the UP would not have hired me if they didn't think I could do the job." She peeked at his badge. "Ken Smith, *Detroit Free Press*. Do they not have women in Michigan, Mr. Smith?"

"She got you there, Smith." The man to her left guffawed and clapped her on the back. "Good one, sister."

Her hat shifted, and her skin burned where he'd made contact. Like an exuberant puppy, his grin was sloppy, the look in his eyes, vacuous. Apparently, he had no idea about his strength or appropriate behavior, but he seemed harmless, so she forced a smile and settled into her seat. At least, all the men weren't misogynistic boars.

Smith mumbled and turned to the guy on his right who gave her an appraising glance before ignoring them both.

With a shrug, she dug into her pocketbook and pulled out a pencil and notepad. Flipping to a clean sheet, she scribbled brief descriptions of the room and its inhabitants. Tension in the room became palpable as the minute hand on the large brass clock ticked closer to the hour.

Known for being loathe to give press conferences, Winston Churchill had agreed to a short forum. What sort of news would he share? With each new month, the Allies secured more ground and captured thousands of surrendering Germans. So much for Hitler's Thousand-Year

Reich. His empire was crumbling, but reports indicated the fighting was more ferocious than before, like a wild animal in pain.

Finished with her notes, she surveyed the room. In addition to herself, there were eight other female correspondents, none of whom she recognized. She sat up straighter and squared her shoulders.

Leaning against the wall, close to the stage, an ebony-haired man with ice-blue eyes stared at her. Movie-star attractive, he had broad shoulders that filled out his charcoal-colored suit jacket. His lips curved in a slow smile.

Her face heated, but Cora refused to look away. She dipped her head, acknowledging his gaze. Which side of the fence was he on? Women stuck at home or out in the world as equals? In her limited experience, the more handsome the man, the more likely he carried an enormous ego. Probably how he managed to get a spot near the podium.

His gaze finally slid past her, and she stifled the urge to turn and see what or who he was looking at. She should be happy he no longer studied her like an insect under a microscope. She pulled at the collar on her blouse. The temperature in the room approached stifling despite the efforts of two aluminum fans. Hopefully, her dress shields would hold.

The door in the front of the room opened. A slight, sixty-something-year-old man emerged, and the conversations ceased mid-sentences. With measured steps, he walked to the stage and positioned himself behind the bank of microphones that nearly obscured his face from the audience.

"Ladies and gentlemen, thank you for your patience. The prime minister has been held up in a meeting and will arrive in approximately twenty minutes. He was to make a short statement then answer a few questions. Questions will not be shouted out, but rather you may submit one question in writing before we begin. Your papers will be collected in five minutes. Please indicate your name and affiliation." A curt nod, then he disappeared through the door.

Cora nibbled the end of her pencil. One question. No pressure there. What was the one thing her readers would want to know about the war? She glanced at the other journalist and caught the handsome reporter staring again. With any luck, this would be the last time she'd see him.

##

Van blinked. He'd been caught studying the woman in the third row. Again. Focus, man. He sighed and glanced at his notebook. Blank. Just like his mind every time he looked at the beautiful reporter. Older than she first appeared because of her petite size, she had an aura of sadness. Her eyes held a cloud of grief. Probably the loss of a loved one, like so many people. A father? A brother? His heart stilled. A husband?

He stole another peek at her. Bent over her notepad, she nibbled on the end of her pencil, giving her the appearance of an intent schoolgirl. What newspaper did she work for? Probably some small weekly in a tiny town. She had tenacity. He'd give her that. Marching to the front of the room and grabbing a seat between the two most irascible guys in the room.

She seemed to be holding her own, oblivious to Smith's glower in her direction. A slight curve to her lips. Maybe she was aware of his unhappiness and had enough spunk not to care. Attagirl.

A teenaged boy emerged from behind the door and walked the aisle collecting questions from the reporters. The young woman nodded to herself, scrawled in her notebook, then tore off the sheet and passed it to the lad. Crossing her arms, she sat back in the chair and stared toward the podium, looking neither left nor right. She seemed to draw a cloak of protection around herself.

The woman had a story.

If this wasn't wartime, he'd take the time to get the scoop. But he was in the middle of a war. No time for romantic entanglements.

The door opened again, and the man who'd made the earlier announcement came out and approached the microphones. The room quieted as only a group of reporters could do when they thought a story was in the making.

"Good afternoon, ladies and gentlemen. Thank you for your patience. As indicated earlier, Prime Minister Churchill will make a statement then answer a select few of your written questions. You will have two hours after the conference to submit your article to the censors. Nothing will be accepted after that time."

Van raised an eyebrow. Churchill was known for controlling information, but what he had to say must be a showstopper and time sensitive. Everyone knew there was going to be an invasion in the next few weeks, but where and when were the best-kept secrets in England. As it should be. Loose lips sink ships and all that.

Commotion near the front, and the rotund head of England's cabinet strode into the room. Although only standing five-feet-eight-inches or so, the prime minister had a presence that rendered him as tall as Roosevelt. Often referred to as a bulldog, Churchill was confident and fearless and more often brash than not. Britain and the Allies were lucky to have him in their camp. Brought in after a vote of no-confidence in Chamberlain's government, Churchill was unpopular with the Conservatives who opposed his replacement of the former prime minister. Surrounding himself with friends and trusted confidantes, Churchill created a cabinet that was the most broadly based in British history.

Thunderous applause filled the room. His political opponents might not like the man, but the journalists loved Churchill. He didn't brook any nonsense, often responding with sarcasm to questions any cub reporter could have devised, but he'd lavish praise for an inquiry that was deep and probing. He might not answer because of national security, but he appreciated a well-researched query.

Churchill raised his hands, and the clapping ceased. Pencils hovered over notebooks waiting to fill their pages. Reporters leaned forward waiting for the erudite speaker to begin. Van straightened, the man's presence creating a desire to stand at attention.

"Ladies and gentlemen of the press, thank you for coming. It is your job to keep our citizens duly informed and to boost their morale. This war has been long and hard, and the conflict isn't over yet. But the great powers of the allied nations will see victory. Of that, I'm sure. The German Army is crumbling, and their leadership running scared, although they will never admit that. We have seen success in Anzio, Bougainville, and Monte Cassino, and we will continue to win battles. As we approach the twilight of this war, there will be many more campaigns during which young men will die, but their deaths will not be for naught. My heart bleeds for every life that is lost, but through their ultimate sacrifice, we will achieve great things."

Holding up his fingers in the familiar V-for-victory gesture, he smiled, his eyes crinkling. Van grinned. Did the man know how charismatic he was?

Churchill continued to speak for another few minutes, his speech a combination of exhortation and innocuous generalities about upcoming campaigns. Nothing that would give the enemy the upper hand but plenty that would tell the folks at home the Allies were confident they would be victorious.

"Now, for questions." The prime minister picked up the top sheet from a stack of mismatched papers. "This is from Cora Strealer, United Press: what strengths have the members of your cabinet brought to the table in Britain's fight against the Axis powers?" Churchill beamed. "A well-formed question, young lady."

As the prime minister answered the query, Van's head whipped toward the woman in the third row whose face glowed pink. Cora Strealer.

Apparently, she had brains in addition to beauty. One more competitor in the ranks.

Chapter Four

Cora stepped into the journalists' room at Broadcasting House. Typewriters clacked and pinged as writers pounded out their stories on an army of machines. Cigarette smoke hung thick in the air. Voices shouted to be heard, and laughter punctuated the buzz of conversation. Her heart hammered in her chest. She had a right to be here, but the scowling, condescending, doubtful faces of the men who watched her every move made her question her confidence.

Would there be a time when women shared the space equally? One woman for every man in the field? Her writing was good, strong. Otherwise, the UP would not have hired her. Did the men not understand that?

She straightened her spine and made a beeline for a vacant machine near the back of the room. Making her way between the tables and chairs, she focused on her destination. No need to see the men's expressions, their disdain was palpable. Did every man in the room feel the same…that she didn't belong?

Her articles would speak for her. Besides, she was here for her readers, not her fellow reporters. They had their jobs, and she had hers. She wasn't looking for friendship in this next chapter of her life.

The past chapter was closed. No longer a wife, but a widow. Brian was gone, buried with his shipmates in the deep waters of Hawaii. What would he think of her new role? Traveling across the globe to take a new job, leaving their friends and her family behind? Would he be proud of her or shake his head in disbelief?

He'd always seemed to support her, but she'd never done anything outside the norm, the rules of society. Then he'd been drafted, and their marriage became a series of letters. She hadn't heard his voice in months when she received the telegram confirming his demise. The days of waiting for confirmation had been interminable. News reports had trumpeted the number of deaths, but the process of identifying the missing and dead had been slow.

Mom and Dad were stunned when she made the announcement of her appointment as a correspondent. They said she always had a place to come home to. Was that because they thought she'd fail? She rubbed her eyes. If she didn't stop wallowing in second thoughts, she'd never get her article written.

The memory of Mr. Churchill's compliment about her question warmed her. At least one man thought she had potential. She shook her head. When had she become so jaded about guys? She would forge her path and ignore the males of the species as Amanda was prone call them. Leaving her friend behind had been the only downside to her move to England. The two of them together would make this assignment a true adventure.

After submitting her piece, she'd write Amanda. Smiling, Cora dropped into the hard wooden chair and laid her notes next to the typewriter. Listening to the hunt-and-peck technique the men on either side were using, she placed her hands on the keys and began to bang out her story, mentally thanking Miss Benedict, her high school typing teacher who drilled her until she could crank out over seventy-five words per minute.

The reporter to her left vacated his chair and another took his place, but she didn't bother to look up. Minutes later, she finished the piece and scanned the words for errors. None. Miss Benedict would be proud.

Cora rolled the sheet from the machine, gathered her notes and pocketbook, and turned to leave. Staring at her from the next station was the handsome reporter from the press conference. So much for never seeing him again. She dipped her head in acknowledgment and squeezed passed his desk.

"Impressive speed, Miss…"

"Strealer. Cora Strealer." He didn't need to know her married name. She was on the job, so she'd use her byline.

"Nice to meet you. I'm Van Toppel, United Press."

"Me too. Are there many of us?"

"Probably, but there's plenty of war to go around." He shrugged. "Where do you hail from?"

"New Hampshire."

"A little late to the party, aren't you?"

"Yes, frankly I was surprised to receive my certification. I wrote for a weekly but was getting mostly fluff pieces. I needed a…uh…change and decided to toss my hat in the ring for an overseas assignment. So here I am."

"Good for you. I—"

A siren shrieked outside.

Cora flinched, and her head whipped around toward the sound. Did Hitler still have enough Luftwaffe to bomb England at this late stage of the war? Eyes wide, she looked at Van.

He stood and grabbed her hand, his palm warm against hers. "Stick close to me. This isn't my first rodeo."

She nodded, and he pulled her close to his side, releasing her hand, and wrapping his arm around her shoulder.

"It will be crowded, but most of the boys are used to the drill, so we should make it to the basement in a few minutes."

Her breath was ragged, and her heart banged against her chest. "It's a drill?"

"No, well, maybe. I was just using an expression. We won't know until later whether the attack is real."

Would she have a coronary before reaching safety? She'd glossed over the liability waiver at the back of the manual she'd been issued. Death seemed far away in the safety of her bedroom. Now, her mortality was inches away. Had Brian known he was going to die? Was this how he felt? She huddled closer to Van as they followed the others down the stairs. How many flights had they descended?

"You're white as a sheet. I guess this is your first air raid. Believe it or not, you'll get used to them."

She shook her head. "I doubt that very much."

They finally reached the basement, and Van led her to a far corner of the room. Benches lined the wall, and she sat next to Van. She didn't normally suffer from claustrophobia, but the dim lighting and dozens of people filling the space made her light-headed. Dizziness threatened to swallow her.

Van pushed her head between her knees and leaned close to her ear. "Take slow, deep breaths. You can get through this."

Her vision cleared, and her face heated. The guy would think she was a shrinking violet. No one else seemed to be panicking. What was wrong with her? She struggled against his hand on the back of her head. "You can let me up. I'm fine." She wouldn't tell him her pulse still raced like a Triple Crown winner.

"You sure?"

"Yes. Thanks for your help." She pulled a handkerchief from her pocketbook and blotted the perspiration at her hairline. "You must think me foolish, but I've never fainted before."

"You didn't pass out." He grinned. "Granted, it was a close one, but you're a real trooper. First raids are the worst."

"Did you faint during your first raid?" She cocked her head and raised her eyebrows in an effort at levity. Interesting that the guy wasn't making fun of her. Was his graciousness genuine?

Van chuckled. "No, but two of my buddies screamed like little girls."

"Ah, but you weren't afraid."

He held up his hands in surrender. "I didn't say that. I said I didn't faint or scream. But I prayed like I'd never done. Bargained with God about everything I'd do for Him if He kept me safe."

"What do they call those prayers? Foxhole conversions?" Cora giggled. Was he a true believer?

"Something like that." Van crossed his arms and leaned back. "We could be here for a while. How about if we get to know each other? I'm from Iowa where my family has been farming since the Homestead Act of 1862. Too many people in this town for my taste, but London is my assignment, so I guess I'm stuck here. What did you do besides write for a weekly in New Hampshire?"

"I think being in the city is exciting. In my tiny town, I rolled bandages, collected scrap, and helped at war bond rallies, like the rest of the women left behind. Not that those tasks aren't important, but I needed to do more."

He studied her, his expression frank and appraising.

Her heartbeat sped up, and this time it had nothing to do with the air raid. Why did he have to be so good looking? She refused to drop her gaze.

Overhead, a muffled explosion rocked the building, and dust showered the room. The group murmured. Cora flinched and grabbed Van's arm.

He patted her hand. "Broadcasting House has made it this far. We'll be fine." His baritone voice was smooth and calm. "Shouldn't be much longer now that the Jerries have hit their target. Then we can get back to work. Well, I can get back to work. Your typing skills put mine to shame. Guess that means you'll be back on the beat before me. Don't grab all the scoops."

Nice of him to try to keep her mind off the falling bombs. She forced herself to breath normally. In. Out. In. Out. "I can't make any promises, Mr. Toppel. A newspaperwoman is only as good as her last story."

"Fair enough." He held out his hand, his expression friendly and without guile. "But when possible, let us UPers keep an eye out for each other."

Cora smiled. Perhaps she'd found a friend after all. She shook his hand, his firm grip sending tingles up her arms. No friend had ever affected her like he did.

Chapter Five

Van pulled his trench coat closed to ward off the chill of the late afternoon breeze as he paced in front of Tewksbury Gun Works. Three days had passed since the air raid at Broadcasting House, and he couldn't purge the attractive reporter from his mind. After the all clear sounded, they'd made their way to a British restaurant near Oxford Circus and grabbed a bite to eat. Interesting how coming close to death whetted his appetite. Or maybe it was time spent with the enigmatic woman.

He'd tap-danced around asking her age, but he'd guess she was only a few years younger than his own thirty-eight years. Faint lines in her porcelain skin bracketed her clear blue eyes, the color of an Iowa sky in mid-June. No matter how much he probed, Miss Strealer wasn't forthcoming about her personal life, other than to say she was the eldest of three girls who also served the war effort.

What was she hiding? Or was she merely someone who valued her privacy? An ironic trait for someone in their field.

Intelligent and witty, she'd shared stories about people from her small town that echoed those from the farming community where his family still resided. Perhaps Cora and he weren't as different as he initially thought.

Deep within the manufacturing plant, a bell rang, indicating the end of the ten-hour shift. He glanced at his watch. Would his informant meet him as planned, or had she changed her mind about blowing the whistle on her employers? Could she afford to lose her job if discovered as the snitch? Was she brave like Miss Strealer? Should he have her talk to the woman?

No. This was his story. He didn't need help…or interference.

He continued to walk back and forth on the sidewalk then forced himself to lean against the streetlight. A more casual appearance than his frantic pacing.

The doors opened, and women poured from the building. Hair put back to rights after being stuffed under kerchiefs and dressed in a rainbow of colors, the women chatted and giggled as they hurried to the bus stop, obviously eager to get home. He searched for the brunette he met by accident at the greengrocer near his boardinghouse.

Shopping late, after opening his icebox to a shriveled apple and miniscule lump of cheese, he'd been scouring the nearly vacant shelves for something he could transform into an easy meal when she approached him. Wearing a fedora pulled low over her face, and a brown wool coat that had seen better days, she'd asked him if he was a reporter, like she'd been told. When he replied in the affirmative, she began to talk, words tumbling from her as if they'd been pent up far too long. She claimed her boss, the accountant at Tewksbury Gun Works, was fixing the books to report more staff members than the company actually employed. She didn't understand how the subterfuge benefited the company, but she knew the activities were wrong.

He suggested she go to the police, but she'd blanched and tried to run out of the shop. He managed to grab her arm and talk her into bringing him proof. A scrap of paper showed up in his mailbox with the plant's address, today's date, and a time of five o'clock. The appointed hour had arrived. Would she?

The flow of employees trickled to a dozen then a handful then none. Van waited a few minutes to see if anyone else emerged. No one. He frowned. So much for the chance at a real scoop. Bad enough to be stuck behind the combat lines when most of his colleagues from home were reporting from the front, but to lose the opportunity to unearth corruption stung. Tewksbury couldn't be the only company trying their hand at war profiteering. How could he sniff out other possible perpetrators? He couldn't very well start quizzing employees from every manufacturer in London.

With a last glance at the brick façade, he trudged to the end of the street toward the White Stag pub. Maybe he could dig up a story among the revelers. He forked his fingers through his hair and turned, nearly plowing into his informant.

Wearing the same coat and hat she'd worn at the greengrocer's, she stood, a folded piece of paper clutched in one hand. She tucked her other hand into the crook of his elbow and tugged him forward. "Eyes are everywhere, Mr. Toppel. Did you really think I'd march out of my employer, cross the street, and hand you the proof? Now, pretend we're having the time of our lives." Her voice was pitched low and terse, then she threw back her head and laughed. "That was a good one!"

He started to look over his shoulder, and she yanked on his arm. "Are you a cub reporter?"

His face heated. She was right about his acting like a rookie. "Sorry. I'm not used to this cloak-and-dagger stuff."

"You'll need to be if you plan to expose these people for who they are." In a fluid motion, she tucked the sheet of paper into his jacket pocket. She smiled and clung to him as if besotted by his presence. "I took a sheet from the back of the ledger, so hopefully no one will notice it's missing. Checking the birth and death records for every name should give you the information you seek."

Van pinned on a smile of his own and spoke though his teeth. "I still think you should go to the police with what you've found."

"Absolutely not. I can't trust the authorities and neither should you. This evil infiltrates levels you can't imagine." The woman leaned close to his ear. "There may be a Pulitzer in it for you. Now, for your protection and mine…" She slapped his right cheek. "How dare you say that! I'm not that kind of girl." Red faced and scowling, she rushed down the sidewalk.

Hand pressed against his stinging cheek, he gaped at her disappearing figure. Katharine Hepburn had nothing on this woman's acting ability.

Bumped by the crowds, he blinked, and shook his head. The hour was too late to begin his investigation, but he'd be at the registry at first light. He had his work cut out for him. Maintaining the farce of jilted lover, he plodded toward the bus stop to head back to his boardinghouse. He had a campaign to plan.

Moments later he boarded the bus, getting the last seat in the crowded vehicle. Countless stops later, he arrived at his lodging, cramped and cranky. Too much humanity for his liking. He headed down the aisle and exited the bus then froze.

Cora sat on his doorstep. Wait. When had she gone from Miss Strealer to Cora in his mind? He rubbed his forehead. He'd think about that later. Much later.

Van approached the entrance, and Cora rose, uncertainty etched on her face. "Are you okay? Has something happened?"

She held out a crumpled piece of paper.

A telegram. He'd recognize the distinctive missive anywhere. His pulse raced. "My family? What—"

"No. This is my telegram, but I thought you received one as well."

"I've been out all day." He snatched the missive from her hand and scanned the words.

NEW ASSIGNMENT WITH VAN TOPPEL. STOP. SERIES OF SIX STORIES DAILY LIFE IN ENGLAND. STOP. OPPOSING PERSPECTIVES. STOP. FIRST ARTICLE FRIDAY DEADLINE. STOP.

"It's from the bureau chief." Van stared at her. "Why would he pair me with you?" He winced at the condescension in his voice.

She frowned. "Why would he think I need to work with you?"

"Touché." He read the telegram again. Maybe his had more information. "I'm already working on a story."

"You can't handle more than one?"

"That's not what I meant."

Cora continued to glare at him, her eyes dark and piercing. "I'm listening."

The more he talked, the deeper the hole he dug. Since when had he become so inept with words? "Okay. Let's start over." He returned the telegram to her and blew out a sigh. "We obviously have no choice about our assignment, so let's figure out the best way to do this without impacting our solo articles. Now, since I've been here for nearly two years, I've got more of an understanding about the deaths and losses experienced by the British people, so I'll take that side of the story—"

"You think you corner the market on grief, Van?" Face dark, she crossed her arms. "How many family members or friends have you lost in the war?"

"Well, uh, none. I guess I've been lucky."

"Yet, you claim to understand what the Brits have been dealing with. I've got news, fella; until you've experienced loss up close and personal, you can't remotely empathize with someone who's lived the pain."

"You—"

"Yes, my husband was killed at Pearl. Sunk on the *Arizona*, so I'll never get him back. How about if you stop making assumptions about my abilities and what I know? Our editor wants opposing viewpoints. I'll take the women's side, and you take the guy's. Then we'll see who has something to report." She whirled and began to stomp down the street then stopped. "No need to interact on the project. Clear?"

"Clear." His face burned as if on fire. What a heel. He'd seen the shadows in her eyes, yet he ignored them, judging her on the basis of…assumptions…like she said. Since when did he do his job based on leaps in logic without conducting research first? Even during his cub reporter days, he hadn't made such a stupid mistake. She had every right to be angry…and hurt. He needed to find her and make amends. Would she give him a second chance? He certainly didn't deserve one.

Chapter Six

A knock sounded at Cora's door, and she jumped up from the couch to answer it.

Sheila, one of the newer girls in the boardinghouse stood in the hallway. Dressed to the nines and heavily made up, the woman had marinated herself in a sickly-sweet perfume. "Cora, there's some guy down in the parlor to see you. A real looker, if you ask me."

"I'm not expecting anyone. Did he give a name?"

"Vic? Vince?" Sheila shrugged. "I was too busy admiring the view to remember. His black hair and blue eyes are quite a combination."

"Van?"

"Yeah. That's it. You know him? Lucky you."

"Not really. My editor stuck me with him on a series of articles, and he's too full of himself for my liking. Jumps to conclusions, and like most guys, doesn't think we gals can do as good a job as they can."

"What a shame. He seemed like a real catch."

"Maybe for someone else." Cora turned and dug out her key from her purse hanging on the coat tree. "Guess I better get this over with."

"Toodles." Sheila wiggled her fingers in farewell, sending another wave of fragrance wafting toward Cora.

"See ya." Cora stifled a cough and locked the door behind herself then hurried down the corridor. Not that she wanted to see Van, but the cloud of perfume was going to choke her to death if she didn't escape. What did the man want?

She frowned. How did he find her? Probably finagled her address from one of the office girls. Score one for the handsome reporter. Ugh. She was as bad as Sheila. He probably knew he was good looking and used his pretty face to his advantage. That would explain his arrogance. Had girls falling at his feet, and when she didn't, he got angry.

Was the opportunity for a byline worth the hassle of collaborating with an empty suit who thought he was better than her? If she was going to make her way in a man's industry, she had to be willing to take a few insults. The other gals did. Women who were more experienced and more famous had to deal with the derision, so she would too. Poor Martha Gellhorn had to regularly remind people she was a reporter long before she became Hemingway's third wife.

Cora stopped in her tracks. Had her editor teamed her with Van Toppel to keep an eye on her, gauge her abilities? Was there something Van knew that he wasn't telling her?

"You okay, Cora?" Hair in braids and wearing a pair of dungarees and an oversized shirt, Wendy Babson stepped out of her room. She looked at her with concern. "You seem upset."

"No. Uh. Trying to figure something out." She gestured to Wendy's outfit. "Problem with your bicycle?"

"Nah. Just doing a tune-up. I put a lot of miles on the bike this week, so I thought I'd give it a look-see. Don't want to break down after dark."

"Amen to that. Hey, you and my sister would get along. She's in the Mechanized Transport Corps, somewhere north of London."

"I've heard of them. Think she would put in a good word for me? I wonder if my luck is beginning to run out. Four years in a munitions factory, and I'm still alive."

"I'll send her a note." Cora shuddered. How could her friend be so cavalier about the danger?

"Thanks." Wendy snapped her fingers. "Drat. I left my tool bag inside. See you around, Cora. I hope things work out for you." She slipped into her room and closed the door.

Cora smoothed her skirt and descended to the foyer then turned left into the parlor where the residents were allowed to entertain male callers. Worn, but still serviceable, the Edwardian-style furniture was arranged in clusters to allow for numerous conversations. Sofas and chairs were upholstered in buttery-soft floral fabric in shades of yellow, dusty rose, and light blue. Myriad small tables held reading lamps.

As she entered the room, Van rose, his brown fedora gripped in his tapered fingers. Tall, with an athletic build, he wore his sport coat with ease. She blinked and cleared her throat. Where was she going with these thoughts? He was the competition, not a prospective date.

A lock of hair fell over his eyebrows that were pinched together. "Thank you for seeing me. I apologize for arriving unannounced. I managed to find out which boardinghouse was yours, but not the telephone number."

"With research prowess such as yours, I find that hard to believe." She smiled to take the sting from her words. "Rather a case of asking forgiveness than permission, Mr. Toppel?"

His eyes widened, and he grinned. "Nothing gets past you, does it, Mrs. Strealer? You're correct. I lied about not having the number, but I wanted to make my apology in person. My behavior was unacceptable, and I'm sorry." He sighed. "And I'm sorry for your loss. The death of your husband must have been…be…devastating."

Tears pricked the backs of her eyes. "Miss Strealer. I use my maiden name for my byline." She cleared her throat and swallowed the lump that had formed. If Brian were still alive, would she be standing in a parlor three thousand miles from home? "Sometimes the three years feel like yesterday, and other times, forever. Thank you for your apology. I'm sure I overreacted. Let's call a truce."

"I'd like that." He nodded and stepped forward, grasping her hand in his. Tingles shot up her arm, and she blinked. Where would their détente lead?

⚬⚬⚬⬥⚬⚬⚬

Van looked at their clasped hands. Her petite palm nestled in his, warm and soft. The heat spread to his elbow, and he released her as if burned. He met her eyes, now clouded with suspicion and hurt. He faked a stumble. "Sorry, I…uh…clumsy. Pardon my clumsiness."

Her gaze cleared, and she cocked her head. "This room is crowded with furniture. Would you like to have a seat? I can prepare some tea, and we can discuss our strategy for the series."

"I'll stay, but I'm a coffee man. Haven't developed a taste for this brown water the Brits call tea."

"I'm afraid I—"

"Oh, no. That wasn't a veiled request for coffee. I'm fine. Nothing to drink, really."

"Okay." Cora gestured toward the ceiling. "Let me get my notepad."

He tossed his hat onto one of the few bare spots on the coffee table and dropped onto the sofa. "I'll be here when you get back."

She hurried from the room, and he stifled the urge to watch her depart. He already knew how well the blue polka-dot dress draped over her trim figure. The clean scent of soap hung in the air. Nice that she didn't drown herself in fragrance like some girls did. He winced at the memory of the young woman who'd let him into the house.

The muted tones of Bing Crosby filtered into the room from the parlor across the hall. A giggle then whispered voices. The record crackled, and Bing sounded as if he'd contracted laryngitis. Van tapped his toe to the rhythm of the music. He was no Fred Astaire or Gene Kelly, but he could hold his own on the dance floor. What would it be like to hold Cora and whirl in a candlelit room, the band serenading them?

Van glanced around. Cora's landlady had done a nice job of decorating. The room was inviting without being too frilly or feminine. He rubbed the cushion beside him. How many guys had sat here wooing women they loved? What was the success rate for the poor fellas?

Footsteps, then Cora appeared in the doorway. Her face was flushed. Had something happened?

"You all right?" He jumped to his feet. "Can I get you anything?"

"No, one of the girls…" She waved her hand. "It's nothing. Let's get started." She lowered herself on the one of the vacant chairs across from the sofa then opened her notepad and turned to a page filled with writing. "I've got a few ideas."

He studied her as she dropped her gaze to the paper. Why had they been teamed together? He'd been writing some far-reaching stories about the war. Had made a name for himself. He wasn't Ernie Pyle or Walter Cronkite, but his articles had touched lives. Letters from readers told him that.

Now, he was shackled to a rookie, albeit a beautiful one. Had she used her looks to get the job? Did she know someone? Why didn't she use her married name? Was she hiding a connection?

"What do you think?" She looked at him, forehead wrinkled.

"I'm sorry, what?"

"My ideas. Did any of them strike you as a good way to start?"

He forked his fingers through his hair, stalling for time. Great. He'd been so lost in his paranoia, he hadn't heard a word she said. Well, he'd do what any professional reporter would do. "They all sound reasonable. Do you have a particular favorite?"

She crossed her arms and glared at him, her lips pressed in a thin line. A long moment passed. "Remember how I don't miss much? Well, it's obvious you didn't hear a word I said. Not sure why you weren't paying attention, but if we're going to work together, I'd appreciate enough respect that you actually listen to me. Thus far, our truce does not bode well."

Face scorching, Van rubbed his forehead. She was right. Again. What was it about this woman that turned him into a stuffed shirt? He was a professional. Why couldn't he seem to act like one? He'd received crummy assignments before. Ones he didn't want to cover, and he'd done them. Without complaint. Yet in the span of two days, he'd insulted his new partner on multiple occasions and couldn't keep his mind on the job. Perhaps it was time to hang up his press pass.

"I'm sorry. You have every right to be upset again." He poked his thumb at his chest. "This isn't who I am. Granted, I'm not the most friendly guy on the beat, but I can work with others. Really."

"I'll try to believe you, but you'll understand if I'm a tad skeptical." She uncrossed her arms and leaned forward. "Look, I'm sure getting saddled with some dame you've never heard of is not your idea of fun. I'd rather do my own stories, too. But we've been put together for a reason the higher-ups think will benefit them, so we need to make the best of the situation. Think you can do that?"

"Yes. Without a doubt. Yes, I can." Why did he feel like a schoolboy in the principal's office? And what was the reason they'd been paired? He'd rummaged up a couple of old newspapers and read her stuff. Her writing was good. Very good. So she didn't need his help. There must be some other explanation. It might take a while, but he'd find the answer.

Chapter Seven

Cora yanked the sheet of paper from the typewriter with a satisfying zip. She scanned the page for errors.

"Hey, Cora." Fanny Detweiler, the only other female correspondent in the room, hollered over the deafening clickety-clack of the machines. "A bunch of us are going to the Fox and Hound. You want to come?"

Laying down the article, Cora shrugged. "I've had a grueling day. How long do you plan to stay?"

"An hour. Maybe two. Come on. It will be fun." Fanny held out her hands. "Help me out. I don't want to be the only gal with these lugs."

"Okay. You win."

Fanny hurried to where Cora stood. "You're a peach. I owe you one."

"No problem. We girls have to stick together. There aren't many of us."

"You got that right." Fanny leaned close. "We've invited that dreamy Van Toppel. I heard you two are collaborating on a series. You're not…you know…seeing each other, are you?"

"What? No!" Cora cringed at the vehemence of her response. She took a deep breath. "I mean, no, and in fact, all we ever seem to do is bicker. He's a condescending know-it-all. Every time he opens his mouth, he insults me. I'll be glad when this assignment is over and done with. You, my friend, may have him."

"He's not that bad, is he?"

"You'll have to judge that for yourself. Maybe it's only me he doesn't like."

"Or perhaps he's afraid you'll outshine him. Face it, Cora, you're a great writer. Someday soon, William Randolph Hearst is going to come knocking."

"I'm not looking for fame, Fanny, but a little acceptance from my colleagues would be nice." Going to a pub with a bunch of cigarette-smoking, misogynistic guys was not in her plans for the day, but perhaps spending time with them would be a way to build a relationship…become one of the boys. Ugh. Just what she wanted. Not.

A few minutes later, she finished correcting her article. Rising from the typewriter, she waved at Fanny who'd gone back to her machine. "Ready." Cora held up her paper. "I need to stop at the censor's office on the way out."

They collected their jackets and pocketbooks, dropped off Cora's article, then headed out of the building.

Cora wrinkled her nose. The pervasive smell of coal never seemed to dissipate. Combined with the fetid exhaust of the buses, the London air was thick with noxious fumes. A chilly breeze lifted her hair and brushed cold fingers across her cheeks. She shivered and pulled her coat closer to her body.

She glanced at the shop as they walked toward the pub. Some windows were crisscrossed with tape to prevent the panes from shattering in the event of an air raid. Other stores hadn't been so lucky as to still have glass. Boards covered their displays with Open For Business painted on the wood. How long would it take for England to recover from too many years of war and destruction?

In the distance a clock chimed four times. Big Ben? She never tired of looking at the iconic tower and often planned her route to take her past the beautiful landmark. Unilluminated at night since the beginning of the war, the clock was damaged during a bombing raid in forty-one. What would it be like to have one's monuments at risk from an enemy?

"Here we are." Fanny stopped in front of a Tudor-style structure huddled between two stone buildings, a nod to the city's nine-hundred-year history.

The pub's wooden sign creaked on wrought-iron hinges as it swung overhead. Cora squinted at the painted board on which a red fox and brown dog each held a tankard. No question as to what the establishment was.

She followed Fanny inside and stopped, waiting for her eyes to adjust to the dimness.

Giggling, Fanny waved at a group seated around a small table. She tugged on Cora's hand, and they squeezed past the crowd huddled at the counter.

Cora's heart banged against her rib cage. Different than the bars at home, England's pubs held a prominent place in its citizens' hearts as a place to socialize and focus on the local community happenings. Would she be forced to drink an alcoholic beverage?

Two vacant chairs awaited them. Fanny jabbed her with an elbow and winked then pushed her into the seat next to Van. Cora swallowed a sigh. What was the girl up to?

She smiled at Van in acknowledgment then lifted her hand in greeting to the other reporters, some of whom she only knew by sight. How important was it to know each name?

"Hello, ladies. What'll ya have?"

Fanny looked coy and gestured to a beer sitting in front of the guy next to her. Tom? Tim? Tony. Name tags would be great.

"Good choice, girly. Let's see if you can hold your liquor."

"Better than you, McCrory."

As one, the journalists cheered as the waitress came to the table. Despite the fatigue lines on her face, the woman smiled and nodded. "Thanks for coming tonight, ladies. What can I bring you?"

Fanny help up her hand. "A beer for me. Cora?"

Cora shook her head. "Uh, do you have anything without…?"

"How about a nice cup of tea, luv?"

"That would wonderful." The tension eased from Cora's shoulders. "You don't mind?"

"Not at all. I'll be back in a jif."

"Tea?" Fanny hissed in a stage whisper. "Really, Cora? How are we going to fit in if you're drinking like a schoolmarm?"

"Mind your Ps and Qs, Fanny." Van's voice rose above the buzz of conversation. "She doesn't have to imbibe if she doesn't want."

Face warm, Cora looked at him and narrowed her eyes. When would the other shoe drop? Only a matter of time before he managed to insult her.

⋯⋯⊶⊷⋯⋯

Van pursed his lips. Cora seemed annoyed rather than appreciative that he'd come to her defense. Not that he expected her to fall on her knees in gratitude, but irritation? She had to be one of the moodiest women he'd ever met. Probably best to ignore her for the evening. Too bad he couldn't avoid her at work.

He shrugged and turned to his left where Harry Medlyn, a writer from Nebraska, hunched over his drink. "Harry, how goes the battle?"

Slight with an elfin face, the journalist could pass for a high school kid. "Just got the word I'm headed to the coast. I leave in the morning."

"A lot going on down there." Van's grip tightened on his drink. Was every other reporter going to get a shot at the big stories but him? "Really? Going to take in some sun and sand?"

"If I get time after covering Ike and the party he's got planned for the Jerries." Harry smirked, looking like a cat who'd unearthed a stash of cream. "Although actually getting a story worth printing past the censors could be a trick."

"Boo hoo. I'm feeling bad for you."

"Sounds like you're going to remain stuck here in the king's backyard? Sorry, old man. You're an excellent writer. Why wouldn't the UP want you where the action is?"

"Guess they think there are still some stories worth writing in the city."

Harry nudged his shoulder. "You'll get a break. Be patient. At least you don't have to worry about making someone a widow."

"Good point. How is the wife? What's new with the kiddos?"

A faraway gaze clouded his friend's eyes. "Martha can ride a two-wheeler now, and Michael got involved in a punch-up at school. They're growing up without me."

"One of the many regrets from this awful war." Van pushed away his mug. "They'll be there when you get home."

"And then maybe I'll exchange my press card for a herd of dairy cows and fields of corn."

"You make that claim about every three weeks." Van grinned. "I'm beginning to believe you. I wouldn't mind doing the same thing. Feeling the earth crumble between my fingers and watching newborn calves stumble to their feet are two of God's gifts. My dad's been holding his own using gals from the Women's Land Army. Said they planted the fields in record time this spring. He can't pay them as much as they'd make with the defense companies, but they don't seem to mind."

"Women at home have picked up the slack, haven't they? Think they even miss us?"

"Now don't get maudlin, Harry. Your missus is counting the days until you walk through the door."

The waitress arrived with a platter of chips, the fried potatoes still sizzling. "There's more where that came from, folks. Eat up."

Van's stomach rumbled at the tantalizing starchy aroma. "The Brits sure know how to do potatoes." He forked a few on his plate as several people around the table did the same thing. Cora reached forward, and her arm brushed his, sending a shiver slithering along his skin.

"Pardon me." Her face pink, she pulled back.

"No need to apologize." He speared a few of the succulent wedges onto her plate. "It's every man for himself, but allow me." Nice to see she had thawed since he first sat down.

"Thanks." She licked her lips. "And thanks for earlier, you know, after what Fanny said."

He tore his gaze from her perfectly shaped mouth. "My pleasure. No one should be told what to believe. Kind of why we're fighting this awful war, on a larger scale, anyway. Freedom from tyranny."

She cocked her head. "Sort of like every man for himself?" A teasing smile lit up her face.

"Something like that." He chuckled. "Do you ever think about what life would have been like if Hitler hadn't started this war or the Japs joined in? Where you'd be or what you'd be doing?"

"Not often, because as terrible as this conflict is, I'm being afforded opportunities I never would have had." She gestured around the table. "Three thousand miles from home doing a job I would not have gotten if I was home. Might not seem like a big deal to you, but for this girl from New Hampshire, it means a lot."

"No one will be the same after this is over." He nodded. "And it is a big deal. At home, I'd be writing about the latest advancements in farming. Not exactly Pulitzer Prize-winning material."

"Will you go back to the agriculture industry?"

"I'm torn. I love to write, make a difference with the articles I publish, but farming is in my blood. I come from a long line of farmers."

"Perhaps you can do both."

"Maybe." He fiddled with the edge of his empty plate. "But we've got a long way to go. There is still a lot of fight in *der führer*. This big offensive that is rumored needs to be highly successful, and no one is betting the ranch at this point."

"Or the farm."

"Funny."

"Trying to be. Our jobs are so much about death and destruction, I can easily get caught up in despair, wondering if God is paying attention or if He's allowing this nightmare as part of some sort of judgment?"

"God? Are you a believer?"

Her face fell. "Yes, but some days, my faith hangs by a thread."

Van's breath hitched. A fellow Christian. As beautiful on the inside as she was on the outside. He was going to have his work cut out for him to remain aloof.

Chapter Eight

Van sat beside Cora on the bus and watched her in his peripheral vision. Two days had passed since the night at the pub when he'd discovered she was a believer. They'd remained at the table long after the other reporters made their exit. Her confession about struggling with her faith put a crack in his armor, and he shared his own doubts. They explored each other's background, tentatively at first, then in a torrent as if knowing time was limited. She'd been through a lot and claimed to be mired in confusion and timidity, but he knew differently. Her strength of character and integrity was evident from the glint in her eye and tilt of her head.

A stray lock of her blonde hair had come undone from her upswept hair, and he stifled the desire to tuck it behind her ear. He was falling for her, and that would never do. He had a career to pursue, and so did she. Friendships were difficult enough during wartime, let alone a romance. Granted, Hitler and his army were on their last legs, but the conflict could easily last another year, maybe more. And eventually, he'd get transferred to the real action. He didn't need strings tying him to London.

Worse, Cora might get killed.

He rubbed his burning eyes. Sleep had been elusive last night, but he finally succumbed to a fitful night of dreams in which he alternately ran for his life or huddled with the masses in a Tube station during a bombing raid and waiting for the all-clear siren. He'd awoken more tired than when he lay down.

Cora, on the other hand, looked refreshed and rested, her fair skin smooth and glowing. Despite her grief and age, she exuded an unexpected näiveté. Wide eyed, she watched the other passengers and the blur of scenery out the grimy, soot-covered windows, seemingly oblivious to his stare.

The bus chugged to a halt at yet another stop. At this rate, it might have been faster to walk across the city to their destination. He withdrew his notebook and flipped it open to his scribblings about their topic: England's orphans and the facilities where the poor urchins were housed. Would their visit have a Dickensian flavor?

He sighed.

Cora turned. A frown creased her forehead. "Is everything all right?"

"Just antsy. And frankly, not too keen on our assignment. There is a huge offensive coming, and I'm covering children. I'm not ungrateful for the job, but…" He closed his pad and shoved it into his breast pocket. Why was their first story an orphanage, of all things?

"Now you know how I've felt most of my career." Her smile was tight. "Listen, every story is important, and when people tire of reading about the killing and the wounding, they'll read our piece about the living. And you never know where an article will lead."

"Well said."

"But?"

"But nothing." He fiddled with his sleeve and cleared his throat. "Let's review the plan. I'll interview the director and get the skinny on funding, logistics, and the business side of the system. You'll talk to the staff and kids. Especially the kids. Hopefully, the younger ones won't have learned to lie."

"Why would they lie?"

"One of two reasons: the administration told them to, or they think they'll get in trouble for telling the truth."

"Have you uncovered information in your research that leads you to believe there are problems?"

"Where there is government aid, there's the opportunity for misuse."

"A rather jaded philosophy." She nudged his shoulder. "Leave your bias at the door, Mr. Toppel."

He bit the inside of his cheek. Who was she to tell him what to think? "Didn't you see those stories from home where corporations were taken to court for mishandling their federal war contracts?"

"Yes, but let's not paint everyone with that brush."

"I'm not…okay…well, maybe I'm skeptical. In any case, I approach my stories with possible angles, then probe the interviewees to see which direction to go."

"As do I…" She waved her hand in dismissal. "Never mind. You handle your side of the investigation as you wish. I'll take care of mine."

Van swallowed another sigh. Offending her was becoming a regular event. What was it about her that made him constantly put his foot in his mouth by being overbearing? As if he had something to prove. "I keep breaking our truce. Forgive me. Unfortunately, I've seen too much, which makes me suspicious, especially if something seems too good to be true. Let's talk about home or a topic less…contentious."

"Fair enough." She grinned. "Do you have a girlfriend?"

"What?" He gaped at her then saw the twinkle in her eyes. She was teasing, knowing full well she'd get a rise out of him. "Oh, funny. As if my love life is not a testy subject."

"Sorry. I couldn't resist. If it makes it any easier, I don't have a boyfriend."

He chuckled. "Good to know. How about you? Any kids? Pets? Long-lost relatives?"

Her gaze darkened for an instant then cleared. "No kids. We…uh…tried, but no success. I suppose that's a good thing now that he's gone."

"Perhaps, but I sense regret." He squeezed her hand. "I'm sorry for the loss of your husband…and the loss of what might have been."

Cora blinked away the sheen in her eyes. "I think that's the worst of it. The what ifs. The speculation. And everyone has an opinion." Her voice hardened. "But despite being married for nearly three years, we were separated for much of that time. Brian was a military man. He was away on assignments, then the war came. And we were separated forever."

He was a writer, yet the words that came to mind seemed contrived, pointless, empty. "I don't know what to say."

"At least you're honest. My friends and family said too much. About how I should feel, what I should do…it was awful. That's one of the reasons I decided to come overseas. Sure, I could have sought a job on another stateside paper, but I needed to do something out of character, to shed the old me." She blushed. "Seems silly and irresponsible now that I've said it out loud."

"It's not. You're a smart and brave woman. Don't let anyone else tell you differently."

Her face lit up. "I appreciate that. When I told my folks about joining the UP, they claimed Brian would not want me to."

His chest tightened. What kind of parents used a dead husband against their kid? He wanted to make her smile as often as he could. Laugh too. "What do you think?"

"I honestly don't know. Like I said, we didn't spend a lot of time together. There are days my marriage seems distant and surreal, almost as if it didn't happen."

Brakes squealing, the bus lurched to a halt. The doors popped open with a hiss. "Glouchester and Cromwell."

Van blinked and climbed to his feet. Where had the time gone? "This is us."

Cora gathered her pocketbook and slid out of the seat.

He gestured for her to precede him, and they clomped down the aisle and off the belching vehicle. A pewter-colored cloud swirled as the bus chugged away. He coughed and covered his nose and mouth. He jerked his head toward the three-story stone house hunched between a church and butcher shop.

"Great location. Feed their souls and fill their stomachs." Cora shouted above the traffic noise.

"Ha. I had the same thought."

They knocked, and a moment later the door swung open. A pencil-thin woman of indeterminable age studied them, her mouth set in a slash. She peered over her glasses. "May I help you?"

Cora nodded. "Yes, ma'am. This is Van Toppel, and I'm Cora Strealer. We have an appointment with Mr. Yorke. We're with the United Press and want to share your good work with our readers."

Van swallowed a grin. He had to hand it to Cora. The woman was making him quake, yet Cora seemed undeterred.

The woman's icy glare gave way to doubt. "You say he's expecting you?"

"Yes, ma'am." Cora extended her arm. "What you're doing here is so very important. The children are lucky to have you, Miss…"

"Mrs. Elton. I'm the girls' housemother." Her expression softened. "Mr. Yorke is the director and handles the boys." She stepped back and motioned for them to enter.

The interior was sparsely furnished, but clean and tidy. A parlor to the left held a Victorian-era sofa and several chairs. The walls were lined with shelves that overflowed with books. Van's eyebrows rose. "How did you secure so many books?"

Mrs. Elton finally thawed, and a smile tugged at her mouth. "Mr. Yorke is a persuasive man and well connected. These volumes came from all over London. With so many schools closed, we hold classes here for our children as well as those in the vicinity. Reading is an integral part of our curriculum."

"Commendable."

"Ah, Mr. Toppel. Miss Strealer. How nice of you to come." A short, rotund man wearing a brown tweed coat and gold spectacles descended the stairs. "I thought we'd start with the children. They've taken a break from their studies and are outside playing."

Van gulped. He'd never been good with kids, and now he was going to be surrounded. "Are you sure that's safe?"

"We haven't lost one yet."

They followed the director through the corridor to the rear of the house. He opened the door to a flurry of activity. A couple of kids squatted over a game of jacks while several kids played catch with a lopsided ball. A group of boys took turns on a tire swing, and a trio of girls skipped rope.

A tiny lad who appeared to be about five or six years old raced toward Cora and wrapped his arms around her legs. She tousled the boy's hair then bent for a quick hug before releasing the child. He grinned and grabbed her hand. "Come."

She glanced at the director who nodded, a wide smile on his face. "Seems you've got a new friend."

Van crossed his arms as she followed the boy to a spot in the yard where a circle had been drawn in the dirt. Apparently, uncaring of soiling her clothes, she sat on the ground next to him. He pulled a handful of marbles from his pocket and put them in the circle. Cora clapped her hands, and the child said something Van couldn't hear.

"Your colleague is special. Warren's been with us for about six months. Lost both his folks in a fire, and he hasn't smiled since he arrived, let alone be willing to embrace someone."

"She suffered her own loss; perhaps he's perceptive enough to recognize a kindred spirit."

"Indeed."

Warren demonstrated how to shoot the marble, knuckles down, thumb flicking the tiny glass ball into the circle. He retrieved the marble and handed it to Cora, motioning for her to give it a try.

Hunched on the ground, her tongue peeping out between her lips, she shot the orb into the ring, missing the other balls. Laughing, she winked at Van over Warren's head.

Van widened his eyes then grinned. Cora had missed on purpose. His heart tugged. She'd make a great mother someday. If she got out of England alive. He had to make sure that happened.

Mr. Yorke clapped him on the back. "Seems Warren isn't the only one who has a special friend."

"No. It's not like that. We're coworkers with the UP. Nothing more."

"My apologies. I guess I misread the situation."

Van tugged at his bottom lip and shrugged. Perhaps not.

Chapter Nine

Cora's fingers flew over the typewriter keys as she pounded out her story about the orphanage. Words poured out of her as she relived the delightful afternoon spent with the children. Van had been skittish around the kids but eventually agreed to a game of catch with two of the older boys. She hadn't probed the reasons for his apparent nervousness, but his behavior intrigued her. He sought an assignment in the midst of battle, yet the presence of youngsters seemed to strike fear in him.

She'd never considered herself nurturing, but playing with the kids had seemed the most natural activity in the world. They'd accepted her as one of their own, especially the darling, little Warren. Hurt and confusion clouded his eyes, but by the end of their time together, the stiffness in his posture had eased, and his expression was less guarded. She couldn't imagine how the children felt, being all alone.

Her heart tugged. What would her own child have looked like? Petite, blonde, and blue-eyed like her or wiry and dark like Brian? Or some sort of combination of them both? Did she wish they'd been successful in having a child before he died? She slumped in the chair and pressed her hand against her chest. Did she regret not having Brians's son or daughter or was she relieved not to be raising a child as a single parent? Would she have resented the child? Felt trapped?

So many questions and no answers.

"You okay, Cora?" A frown creasing her forehead, Fanny sat at the typewriter next to her. "You look upset. Something in your story got you down?"

Cora sighed and smoothed her skirt. "No. Well, the article got me to thinking."

"About?"

"My life." She cleared her throat. "I'm writing about my visit to the orphanage, and the next thing I know, I'm ruminating about the fact Brian and I didn't have kids, and what all that means. Everyone has kids. Why didn't we?"

"I don't share your faith, but maybe that God of yours knew saddling you with a kid as a widow wasn't fair."

"Or in His plans. I hadn't thought of it like that before."

"Do you really think He lays out your life like a movie script?"

"No, because we have free will to make choices, but He definitely has things He wants me to do."

"Whatever you say." Fanny cocked her head. "Do you think He wants you to get married again?"

Van's image flashed through Cora's mind, and her face heated. What was that all about? Too many incidents of bossiness and condescension outweighed the few lighthearted moments of camaraderie. She frowned. "If He does, He hasn't sent any likely candidates."

"What about—"

"Don't finish that sentence. For about a million reasons, my coworker is not a good choice. But you know I was older than most women when we wed. I was single and on my own for a while before meeting Brian. I don't need to have a husband to be complete. Besides, women are forced to stay home after getting married. I love my job and want to continue a career in journalism after this war. Don't you?"

"I guess. To be honest, I haven't really thought about married life and what that means for me." She batted her eyelashes. "I'm not interested in tying myself down with one guy at this stage. Especially somebody from home. That'd be boring, and the last thing I want is a humdrum life."

Cora chuckled. "Yeah, boring and you definitely don't go together."

"It's not fair that we women don't have as many choices."

"No, but the war has changed society. Think about it. During the Great War, there were only a few female reporters, and they were tasked with covering the woman's side of the war, but only if their magazine or newspaper sent them. The military refused to accredit gals back then. Now, there are a bunch of us, and we're managing to get where the action is."

"By hook or by crook."

"True, but thanks to Dickey Chapelle, Margaret Bourke-White, and Martha Gellhorn, we're in the big leagues now. Our bylines are next to the boys' bylines, and they can't say anything about it."

The door opened, and Van sauntered in, jacket slung over his shoulder. Hair in disarray, his face was lined with fatigue. Or was it worry? Where on earth had he gone after they finished at the orphanage? His gaze swept the room, then touched on her, and his eyes shuttered. What was going on?

"There's your partner now."

Cora snorted a laugh. "A word suggesting collaboration. Not happening."

Fanny raised her eyebrow. "What's he doing now?"

"Later. I don't want to be overheard." She gestured to the paper still locked in the machine. "Besides, I need to get this finished so I can submit it to the censors. I understand the need for review, but the added step shortens my deadline."

"Good luck." Fanny pulled her piece from the roller and stood. "I'm off. Meet me at the pub at nine o'clock. I want the whole story." She raised her hand. "Van, I'm done over here if you need a machine."

He waved and kept talking to a pair of writers from the *Detroit Free Press.*

"Fanny—"

"Ta ta." Her friend threaded her way through the row of desks, hips swinging, and more than one man watching her grand exit.

Cora rolled her eyes. That girl was going to be the death of her. Pushing Van at her after hearing about his attitudes and behaviors was a dirty trick. She'd have to come up with a way to get back at her.

The trio of men guffawed, their laughter puncturing the sound of the typewriters, and Cora peeked at them from under her bangs. Of the three, Van was definitely the most handsome, but even though he was a believer, he treated her as a subordinate, someone of less value. That kind of bias made him objectionable. She pressed her hand against her wrist and thinned her lips. She'd have to remind her racing pulse of his unsuitability.

⚬⚬⚬●⚬⚬⚬

Van watched myriad emotions play across Cora's face before her expression became impassive, and she bent her head over the page in her machine. She'd managed to dismiss whatever was bothering her.

He'd heard enough of the reporters' complaints. Time to get a jump on his story and see how Cora was coming along with hers. Would she let him read her piece, or would she interpret his interest as interference? Probably the latter.

With a final nod to the guys, he excused himself and made his way to the vacant typing station next to the lovely yet enigmatic journalist. He dropped into the chair and rolled a sheet of paper into the machine.

Her body seemed tense after he sat, so he focused on his work. After a few aborted starts, he immersed himself into the story.

Van reached the end and sat back with a sigh. The words had flowed as if being dictated. He'd woven some of his own history into the piece, and now memories flooded his mind. He rubbed his burning eyes and waved away the fetid cigarette smoke that encompassed the room. A nasty, prevalent habit practiced by a large percentage of society.

"Seems inspiration struck." Cora's voice was soft and melodic. "Are you pleased with the results?"

He blew out a deep sigh. "Yes, I'll have to proof the piece, but it feels good. Complete. I think I was able to infuse the human interest side into the documentary-type stuff that can be kind of dry. Necessary, but boring if I'm not careful."

"Mind if I look at it? I'd like to see how our styles mesh." She held out a sheaf of papers, a tentative look clouding her eyes. "Only if you want to, of course."

"A great idea." He pulled the last sheet from the typewriter, put it on the bottom of his stack, and laid the pile on her table, then took her pages. "Not that we want to mimic each other's way of writing but knowing how we approach a topic will be helpful."

His palms slicked with moisture. What would she say when she discovered he was an orphan? Would she look at him with pity? Scorn? No. Disdain wasn't her way.

She picked up the document and began to read.

Rather than read her essay, he nibbled his lower lip and studied her expression. Conversation ebbed and flowed, mingling with the clatter of typewriter keys and the ping of the carriage-return bell. Time seemed to stand still while he waited.

Finally, when he didn't think he could wait another minute, she laid down the last sheet and turned toward him, something akin to wonder on her face. Not the emotion he'd anticipated.

"You've written a powerful story, Van. The inclusion of your own situation while growing up adds credibility. Not that you need it with your reputation as a reporter, but I'm just an observer. In a sense, you've walked in these kids' shoes." She smiled, a gentle, accepting curve to her mouth. "Hopefully, one day I'll be half the writer you are. Thanks for letting me read it. I wouldn't change a thing, and I didn't see anything that would raise flags with the censors."

The tightness in his chest eased, and he returned her smile. Her words meant a lot. More than he thought possible.

"I'm sorry for your loss. Even though you had your grandparents, growing up without a mom and dad must have been difficult."

He nodded and swallowed against the lump that had formed in his throat. "Being raised by my dad's parents made me different, and you know how mean kids can be. Nana and Pops were quite a bit older, the only gray-haired people in the audience for school plays, choral concerts, and baseball games." He frowned. "I wasn't very nice to them."

She squeezed his arm, and tingles warmed his skin. "How old were you when your parents passed?"

"Eight. They died in a train accident in Colorado. Dad had secured a new job out there, and they went ahead to make housing arrangements." He rubbed at the crease on his slacks. "I was angry for a long time, bitter. Those emotions didn't make for a very nice kid. My grandparents did the best they could."

"They had their own grief to contend with."

"Exactly."

"Are they still…?"

Van shook his head. "No. They passed a couple of years ago, but not before we made our peace. I'm grateful for everything they did for me, and I was sure to let them know." Why was he pouring his heart out to this woman? And why did it feel so right?

"You're a good man, Van Toppel."

"Remember that the next time I annoy you." He grinned and cocked his head. "Deal?" He extended his arm. "I imagine agitating you won't take long."

A playful smirk on her face, she shook his hand. Her laughter, silvery and bell-like swirled around him. "I look forward to it."

What would it be like to make her laugh every day? Maybe even into their old age? Whoa. Where did that thought come from? They were colleagues. Nothing more. Life was too precarious during wartime, possibly snuffed out at any moment. He did not need the complications associated with a romance, but his thudding heart was not cooperating with that knowledge.

Chapter Ten

Cora took a deep breath, then coughed, the exhaust fumes and smell of coal invading her nose. She'd been caught up in the beauty of the day with its cloudless sky and birdsong, and managed to forget about the smoggy city air. Foolish move.

"Are you okay?" Van leaned forward, concern lining his face. "We could go inside the café."

"I'm fine, but wishing I was in New Hampshire where the air smells clean. How do people live here? Especially before the war when there was more motor traffic?"

"They don't know any better." He offered his handkerchief. "I wouldn't mind being in Iowa. The crowds are what get me. Too much humanity sometimes." He shuddered. "And when I have to stuff myself into a Tube station or other shelter during a bombing raid. Ugh."

"Besides the open spaces, what do you miss about home?"

"Easy question…the leisurely pace. Don't get me wrong. I love to chase a good story as much as the next reporter, but rising with the sun and walking the fields before leaping into the day seems to ground me." He flushed and ducked his head. "Does that sound like a ridiculous thing for a grown man to say?"

"Not at all. Tell me about Iowa. I've never been."

"The state is very different from your mountainous New Hampshire. We have some rolling hills, but as part of the Great Plains, most of the landscape is flat. A person can see for miles. Years ago, I was heading to town from Dad's farm, and I could see something in the road. About forty minutes later, I finally drew abreast of the object, and it turned out to be some hay bales that had apparently fallen off someone's truck."

"I can't imagine what that's like. With all the lakes in New Hampshire, our roads twist and turn. A driver is lucky to see more than a quarter mile ahead."

"I visited New Hampshire for the presidential primary during the election of thirty-two. One of my first big assignments outside of Iowa. So different than what I grew up with, but just as pretty."

Cora blanched. He'd been to her state. Walked where she'd walked. What would it be like to go home and follow his footsteps?

"More tea, miss?" The waitress hovered at Cora's shoulder. "Something to eat?"

Her stomach rumbled, and she pressed her hand against her middle. Face heating, she nodded. "Apparently, I'm hungry."

Van chuckled, and she glared at him.

He held up his hands in surrender. "Sorry."

"Whatever you've got is fine."

"Cucumber sandwiches coming up. The owner got a produce delivery."

Cora brightened. She'd eaten her weight in canned food. Fresh vegetables would be a treat. "Let's review the ideas we've come up with thus far. Maybe one of them will jump out as the next great story."

"First—"

"Cora Strealer, is that you?" A strident voice split the air.

Cora flinched. She'd know those tones anywhere. Her shoulders knotted, and she clenched her hands into fists, fingernails biting in her palms. She refused to turn toward the sound. Let her nemesis come to her. Van looked at her, questions written all over his face. He'd find out soon enough.

Footsteps clattered on the sidewalk. "Cora!" The woman's nasal voice carried like a foghorn on the coast of Maine.

Tall and willowy, Myrtle O'Malley arrived at the table, dressed to the nines as if she were headed to a cocktail party. Mahogany hair swept into a smooth chignon with eyebrows tweezed into perfect arches, she nudged Cora then held out her hand to Van, who ignored the gesture. "Who have we here? Does Brian know about this little tête à tête?"

"He's dead, Myrtle. You know that." Cora spoke through gritted teeth. "This is Van Toppel, a colleague from the UP. What are you doing over here?"

Seemingly unfazed by Van's response, Myrtle grabbed a chair from one of the nearby tables and shoved it between Cora and Van before dropping onto the seat. She batted her eyelashes at Van. "You're right. His death must have slipped my mind. I guess that's why you're able to gallivant around London with this handsome man."

"I'm not on a vacation. We're working together on a series of articles. Why are you in London?"

"Haven't you heard? I'm with *Collier's* now, and they've sent me all over Europe. I'm back in the city to see what I can ferret out about the big campaign in the works." She nudged Van's shoulder and wiggled her eyebrows. "What are you two 'collaborating' on?"

Van pulled away, and Cora stifled a grin. Apparently, this was one man who wouldn't fall prey to Myrtle's charms. Unlike Louis, the young man who'd asked Cora to marry him, then broken the engagement only to be dumped by Myrtle three months later when she'd tired of him.

"Confidential, Myrtle. You know that. Just because you blurt out your assignment doesn't mean we have to share ours."

"Well, la-di-da. No need to be snooty, Cora. Are you still sore because Louis chose me over you?"

"Actually, no. If I'd married him, I wouldn't have met Brian." Cora narrowed her eyes. "Are you still sore that I bested you out of the job in Lakeport?"

Myrtle's face darkened for a flash before her simpering smile settled in place. "Clever jibe—"

"As interesting as this reunion is, Miss O'Malley, we're on deadline. I'm sure you understand. Maybe we can meet you at one of the pubs later."

"That would be lovely. Perhaps we can discuss possible collaboration between ourselves, Mr. Toppel. I'd make a great addition to UP's cadre of writers."

"I don't—"

She held her index finger to his lips. "Shh. Later. We'll discuss this exciting opportunity later." She glanced at the jeweled watch pinned to her jacket lapel. "The Fox and Hound at…say…eight o'clock. Don't feel like you need to join us, Cora."

Heart hammering in her chest, Cora smiled sweetly. "Oh, but I don't want to miss the chance to catch up with you."

Myrtle's smile faltered, then she rose and bent to lay a kiss on Van's cheek. "I look forward to seeing you again." Without a backward glance, she minced away on teetering stiletto heels. The scent of *Evening in Paris* clinging to the air around them.

Van blew out a breath and sagged in his chair. "Wow, that's one predatory woman. She scares me."

"Truth be told, she frightens me, too." With a shaky laugh Cora pushed away her teacup. "I guess you got the gist of our…uh…relationship. And now it appears she wants my job and my partner. I can't believe I've come over three thousand miles to be stuck with her in the same city. What are the odds?" She rubbed her forehead then dropped her hands into her lap. Van didn't seem to be affected by her act, but Louis hadn't been either at first. How long before Van became snared in the woman's web?

Van squeezed her arm. "Hey, don't allow her to get under your skin. You have a lot of history, and she's obviously hurt you, but I won't let her do that again. We need to get ahead of any subterfuge she might be arranging now that she knows you're here."

"She has been a thorn in my side since college. Stealing my boyfriend just to see if she could was the least of her crimes. I'm not sure what she thinks I did to her, but she's had a vendetta against me from our first class together. She went out of her way to undermine me with my professors and tried to get me into trouble with the administration. After college, we ended up at the same newspaper, and she tried to get my editor to believe I'd plagiarized one of her articles. Fortunately, I had all my notes and was able to prove her false."

"Bet that didn't sit well."

"No, and then I was promoted. Shortly after that she moved to a different paper, not sure which one." She shrugged, her bunched shoulder muscles protesting the action. "Maybe that's when she landed at *Collier's*. Anyway, how will you put the kibosh on her shenanigans? She's a climber and will do whatever it takes to get an article, a scoop…or a man."

"I'll send a telegram to our editor in case she tries to contact him with claims of our recommendation. Then we'll do what we do best and write our stories, keeping a very close eye on Miss O'Malley. We're in this together. Partners, like you said."

Tension seeped from Cora's back, and she blinked away the moisture that had sprung to her eyes, unbidden. When was the last time she'd had this kind of support? Long before Brian had left for Pearl with a promise to return.

Could she trust Van? Was he truly changing as he'd indicated he was trying to do, or would he slip back into his chauvinistic attitudes leaving her alone to deal with Myrtle? She'd handled her adversary in the past on her own, but having Van beside her, looking at her like he was, acting like he cared…she could get used to that.

Chapter Eleven

Cora hurried to keep up with Van's long strides as they made their way to the police station. Shopkeepers from two stores in Marylebone on the west end of London had been arrested on charges of involvement in the black market. Van had called in a favor with one of the detective inspectors for an interview. Later, she would track down the merchants' customers for their side of the story.

She shook her head. Why did people take advantage of others during difficult times? Did the men have no consciences? Life was hard enough with loved ones in the armed forces, bombing raids, and other stressful situations. Citizens should be pulling together, not giving in to greed.

Debris on the sidewalk crackled under her feet. Would London never be clean again? How long would it take the residents to rebuild their homes and businesses when all was said and done? America was blessed that she hadn't suffered as badly as the countries on this side of the globe. Ships had been sunk, and there'd been a few incidents with subs, perhaps more than she'd know about in her lifetime, but all in all her country was safe from marauders.

Blinking away the morbid thoughts, she grabbed Van's arm. "Do we have to run the entire way?"

He slowed his pace, and his face reddened. "Sorry. I was rehearsing the questions I want to ask."

"As a good reporter should." She smiled. "I do the same thing. Did you come up with some good ones?"

"I think so." He leaned close to her ear, his breath caressing her cheek.

Trembling, she tried to focus on his words, not his proximity.

"I'm going to try to get DS Graham to let us speak to the prisoners."

She stopped short. "What a great idea. We'd get insight into their motivation. Maybe it's not all about the money for them. Do you think he'll allow that?"

"Doubtful, but worth a shot." Van motioned toward the brick building about thirty yards away. "We're here." He winked. "Maybe you can use your beauty and feminine charm to get permission."

"I'm not sure how to take that." She grinned. "But since I'd love to get the chance to speak with the perpetrators, I'll overlook any possible insults."

He held up his hands in surrender. "No insult intended. You are a great writer, but sometimes we journalists have to get…um…creative in getting to our sources. And since you're a lot prettier than I am, you have a better chance of swaying the detective inspector."

"If he's shallow and petty."

"We can only hope."

She rolled her eyes. "Or we can appeal to his sense of the importance of understanding the motivation of these people."

"Have it your way." He tucked her hand into the crook of his elbow. "The game is afoot, Watson…er…Strealer."

Her giggle died in her throat. Myrtle stood at the entrance of the police station. What was she doing here? Was she chasing the same story? How had she heard about the arrest?

Cora glanced at Van who seemed as surprised as she was to see the woman, so her niggling concern that he was in contact with Myrtle was nothing more than mistrust and worry. Van was not underhanded. He was a lot of things, but lying and subterfuge weren't some of them. She crossed her arms and pressed her lips together. Did the woman really think batting her eyelashes was effective? *Lord, help me not lose my temper. Help me see her from Your perspective.*

Van squinted and shielded his eyes. "Miss O'Malley. A pleasure to see you again." His tone belied his words. "To what do we owe the honor?"

"Trying to get a story, same as you." She sauntered toward them, hips swaying. "No success yet, but if you're here, there must be something I'm missing."

He shrugged.

"Won't you give me a hint?"

"Journalists worth their salt, don't reveal their secrets. Surely you know that, Miss O'Malley."

"A girl can try, can't she?" Myrtle stroked Van's arm. "After all, we're colleagues."

"Actually, we're not. Fellow reporters, yes, but we work for rival news organizations. I'm not willing to lose my job for you, Miss O'Malley."

The woman's ingratiating smile slipped into a frown, and she stepped back. "Understandable, *Mister* Toppel. But we'll meet again, and I will scoop you." She whirled and marched down the sidewalk, spine stiff.

Cora refrained from cheering, glad she'd prayed about the interaction. Her human-self wanted to best the woman, show her up and win. But giving in to such earthly desires would turn Myrtle away from any chance of believing in God.

Van pulled open the door and motioned for Cora to precede him. "That was a close one. I wasn't sure how we were going to lose her if she followed us inside."

"She's as tenacious as ever." Cora entered, the tile and wood lobby offering cool relief from the sunshine and warmth outside. "What if she keeps showing up where we are? She might scoop us after all."

"We'll cross that bridge, and all that. London is teeming with journalists. There's enough war to go around."

They approached the desk, and Cora fumbled in her pocketbook for her press pass. What was it about the station that brought out her nerves? She wasn't a criminal, but the austere expression of the uniformed officer behind the counter produced feelings of guilt, as if she had something to confess.

Van displayed his pass then scrawled his name on the log. "Good afternoon, Sergeant. Miss Strealer and I have an appointment with Detective Sergeant Graham." His voice boomed. "Would you be so kind as to tell him we're here?"

Cora drew herself to her full five-foot-three-inch height. They had an appointment. Since when did she cower in the face of authority? She grabbed the pen and signed her name with a flourish.

"Yes, sir. The inspector is expecting you, but will be a few more minutes. Follow me." He led them down a narrow hallway then opened a door marked Interrogation Room #1. "Would you care for tea?"

"No, thank you, Sergeant. We're quite comfortable."

"Suit yourself." He closed the door, and his footsteps faded.

Goose bumps raised on Cora's arms, and she rubbed her cold skin. "Interrogation room, huh? Is this his attempt at intimidation?"

"Maybe, but it's more likely he wants us out of the way and unable to see what's happening elsewhere."

She glanced at the dingy, gray walls, one of which held a sign that proclaimed Prisoners Must Remain Seated At All Times. The only window was on the door, and the pane was frosted, preventing her ability to see into the corridor. The stale odor of cigarette smoke and sweat permeated the room. How many prisoners passed over the threshold? How had war impacted the number?

"We might have another story, Van. What if we explored how the war has changed the face of crime? In a time of killing, do men and women break the law more or less often?"

"Brilliant, Cora." Van's face lit up. "Positively brilliant."

She warmed at his words, and her heart skittered. Perhaps this partnership would work out after all.

━━ ••◦●◦•• ━━

Van's chest expanded. Cora beamed at him like he'd just handed her an expensive gift. He blinked. In a way, he had by complimenting her idea. What was it like to be a woman in a man's field? Probably a laborious effort to be accepted as a colleague, someone who could do the job as well as the men.

The women on his home newspaper had covered society events, food, fashion, child-rearing, and other topics geared toward the home. Had any of them wished they'd received tougher assignments? Gritty stories that required deep investigation? Or had they been satisfied with their place on the staff?

More than one hundred women had been certified as war correspondents by the government. Surely, they weren't the only females in the nation who had interests of a worldly nature. He cocked his head. Cora made him rethink everything he'd ever known.

Leaning back his chair, Van pulled his notebook and pencil from his shirt pocket. "Maybe DS Graham will give us a hand with this piece, too. Or he might have connections at Scotland Yard who would be willing to speak with us. We could take the opportunity to shine the light on the work they're doing to keep England safe at home while many of her men are in combat."

Seated next to him, Cora nodded. "We could go into the neighborhoods to conduct interviews too. Find out how men and women feel about their safety, and their perception of the level of crime." She tapped her chin with her index finger. "London has a lot of ground to cover. We'd have to decide how to divide the city in order to get a good cross section of people."

"Merchants, also. They'll definitely have an opinion, especially about black-market business."

Cora tilted her head. "Do you ever struggle reconciling your faith with the amount of evil that seems to be sweeping across the globe? At this stage of the war, it appears the good guys will win, but how many of our allies can we trust? England and America only partnered with Stalin because of a mutual enemy. What will happen when the war is over? Uncle Joe seems like he might try to get more than his fair share of the spoils."

Van rubbed his jaw. "God's plans are difficult to see during times of war and terrible events, when thousands or even millions of people die. When I heard about how many Jews and other so-called undesirables

Hitler had exterminated, I was angry at God for not intervening. Assassination attempts were made on Hitler, yet he was never killed. Why not? I still don't understand why God allowed him to live, but I've learned that I will never know the whole picture." He shrugged. "But I still question God as to why the war raged as long as it has."

"What a relief to know I'm not alone with my doubts."

He pulled at a stray thread on his sleeve. "At least you don't have to wonder if you're hiding behind your typewriter."

Cora straightened. "What do you mean?"

"Face it, I'm a perfectly healthy young…er…youngish man, yet I carry a pen not an M1 rifle. I chase stories, not enemy soldiers, sailors, or air men. Shouldn't I be in uniform putting my life on the line?" He refused to look at her. Seeing her pity or condemnation would be debilitating.

She reached out and stilled his hand, the warmth of her palm sending darts of electricity up his arm. The clean scent of her hair wafted toward him. "If you're saying you're a coward, I disagree."

"But—"

"But nothing. I may not be a military strategist, but maybe the division of responsibilities is like in the church. Paul talks about many members of one body. People have different areas of expertise. Don't hear me say that war is anything like church or the body of Christ, but you have certain gifts. Yes, you could train to be in the armed forces, but I think your skills are better used wielding your pen, not a sword. God calls us each to different tasks. Your writing can impact one person or millions." A gentle smile bloomed on her face. "Do you think all the other correspondents are cowards and should have enlisted?"

"Well, no, but many of those guys are older."

"Yes, but don't you think if the War Department wanted you to serve, you'd have received your draft notice?"

"I did, but when I reported for duty and indicated I was a journalist, I received a waiver. Sometimes I wonder if I should have told them I didn't want special treatment."

"You're saying you know better than the War Department?"

"When you put it like that, no." He blew out a sigh. "Are you just trying to make me feel better?"

"Absolutely not. Haven't I proved myself cantankerous and opinionated?" She giggled. "You'd prefer I didn't spare your feelings?"

He chuckled. She really was a pip. He'd been lucky not to have been saddled with someone like Miss O'Malley. With a shudder, he raked his fingers through his hair. He needed to protect Cora from the woman's machinations. Her actions made it clear she couldn't be trusted not to undermine Cora or try to pull a story out from under her. Would she try to contact their editor with the false claim that they wanted her help? He'd sent the telegram but hadn't received a response. Was he too late?

The door opened, and DS Graham stepped into the room. Tall and broad shouldered, he filled the room. Piercing green eyes stared at them, his mouth set in a slash above a cleft chin.

Beside him, Cora's quick intake of breath was audible. Did she find the man attractive? Van studied her from under lowered eyelids. Would his attempts to thwart Miss O'Malley mean anything to her, change her feelings toward him? Why did that suddenly matter?

Chapter Twelve

"I picked up the articles from the censor's office, and both pieces passed with flying colors." Cora smiled and waved a sheaf of papers at Van as he entered the typing room in Broadcasting House. "I've already transmitted them, and I hope you're interested in grabbing a bite to eat while we discuss the next assignment. I'm starving."

Van rubbed his stomach. "Excellent. We've been so busy this week I haven't been to the market in days. The lone item in my icebox is a shriveled lump of cheese, and the canned meat in my cabinet held no allure this morning. There's a wonderful sandwich shop around the corner."

They hurried downstairs and out of the building.

Cora squinted at the brightness as sunshine warmed her head. "I was pleased at how forthcoming DS Graham was with his comments about crime statistics. Too bad he wouldn't let us speak to the suspected black marketers."

"Not surprising." Van stuffed his hands in his front pockets. "Guess he figures the men might try to garner sympathy through the press. We don't want to make these guys look good."

"What did you think of the detective?" She gave him a sidelong glance trying to read his expression. He'd been alternately standoffish and pushy, almost like his former self when she'd first met him. They barely knew the policeman, yet Van seemed to exude a strong dislike as soon as the man entered the interrogation room.

"A little too enamored with himself, but helpful." He waved his hand as if brushing away a gnat. "I'd rather focus on our next piece than discuss the intrepid detective sergeant."

"Okay, but one question." Cora narrowed her eyes. Van was definitely snippy about the guy. "What gives with you and Graham? Have you met before? Did he say something that angered you?"

"There's nothing between us. He did his job, and we did ours. End of discussion." His nostrils flared. "Now, for the new assignment, I was able to unearth quite a bit of information about the internment camps. We can start with the Parliament's decision to pass the Defence Regulations and invoke section 18B for British nationals. Something called the Royal Prerogative was used against enemy aliens."

Cora looked at him for a long moment. She'd only known him for a few weeks, but her reporter's senses said he was hiding something, and that something seemed related to DS Graham. But Van had made it clear any conversation about the man was finished. So be it. Maybe she'd do some digging of her own. She blew out a sigh. "Fine. We don't want the article to sound like a term paper, but we'll have to give the American people enough background so they'll understand how British government differs from the US."

"What do you think about comparing internment here with that of Japanese, Italian, and German people at home?"

"The contrast would be an interesting study considering the bulk of the internees here have been released while those at home are still being held. My research shows that of the more than seventy thousand people initially confined within Britain, fewer than a thousand still remain in custody."

"I can't imagine how these people feel about being arrested because of their heritage. Lots of the detainees have lived here for decades. Fear and mistrust seem to be the basis for the decisions."

Van frowned. "Not necessarily. I'd say prudence entered into their ruling. Better to be safe than sorry, as they say."

She cocked her head. "Let me get this straight. If my family emigrated from Switzerland to America when I was a child, and the US went to war with the Swiss, we should be arrested and detained because we might be spies."

"That's not a good example. Switzerland is neutral."

"Don't be obtuse. You know the point I'm attempting to make."

"I'm just saying that a country has to make the decision it feels is in the best interests of its citizens."

She threw up her hands. How could he believe the government should be allowed to ignore its taxpayers' freedoms? "But what if some of the folks they detain are citizens? I don't know about here in Britain, but a percentage of the Japanese in the camps aren't just residents. They were born in the US. Look at the 442nd Infantry Regiment comprised completely of second-generation Japanese-Americans. Citizens whose rights have been stripped."

Van's stomach rumbled, and his face reddened. "Apparently, it's time to quit bickering so we can grab lunch." He smiled. "Guess we know that our article is going to create some conversation, huh?"

A giggle slipped out, and she tugged at her skirt. Nice of him to smooth over their words. "So much for me remaining an impartial journalist."

"Nothing wrong with being passionate about your topic." They arrived at the restaurant, and he opened the door for her. "I'll bet you five shillings today's menu is fish."

"Ha. I'm not taking that wager. Fish is about the only plentiful food in England. If I eat any more fish, I'm going to start growing scales and gills." She sobered up. "I guess I shouldn't complain. Fish is better than nothing, and many people around the world are starving."

They made their way to a vacant table, and the waitress arrived seconds later. A young woman of perhaps twenty-five, she had short ginger-colored hair and startling green eyes. Though tired looking, she wore a broad smile. "Some tea for you? We're serving a lovely potato soup with bread."

Cora grinned at Van. "I should have taken the bet after all." She looked at the young woman. "Soup and tea sounds lovely."

"You're Americans." She poked her pencil behind her ear. "How come you're not in uniform?"

"We're journalists with the United Press. Van Toppel and Cora Strealer."

The girl squealed. "Reporters. My name is Molly. Maybe you should interview me." She lowered her voice. "I could tell you all kinds of things I've heard. Waitresses are invisible, and people talk in front of us as if we can't hear them."

Cora exchanged a glance with Van. Did Molly have information of value? Surely, her customers obeyed the directive not to discuss topics of national importance. Loose lips sinking ships as one poster proclaimed.

Van unfolded his napkin and placed the cloth in his lap. "Perhaps after your shift, but for now we'd appreciate our food."

Molly slapped her forehead. "Of course. Shame on me, standing here blathering like you're Clark Gable and Vivien Leigh. I get off work at two o'clock if you decide you want to talk to me." She scooted between the tables and disappeared into the kitchen.

"Likening us to movie stars." Van puffed out his chest and lifted his chin, rubbing an imaginary mustache. "Maybe we should leave her our autographs."

"Don't get too full of yourself, Mr. Toppel." She snickered. "Especially if we question her for our upcoming article about internees.

She could have very strong opinions, and not necessarily ones that agree with yours."

"Like yours." His eyebrow arched high on his forehead.

She shrugged. "I just had a thought. How does the government know they've detained the right people, and by that, I mean the ones who really could be spies or fifth columnists? Someone could change their name, get false papers, and blend into society."

He froze, but the muscle in his cheek jumped.

Was that an indication he was hiding something?

Chapter Thirteen

The train shimmied and bumped over the tracks as it sped south toward London. Van crossed his arms and surveyed his fellow passengers. Most were hidden behind a newspaper while a few stared out the window or slept. Several windows were open, and the acrid smell of coal exhaust swirled through the car.

Next to him, Cora sifted through the notes she'd made while they were at the internment camp. Apparently, someone of importance wanted good press about the conditions of the facility because they'd been given a full tour and an interview with the camp commander, Major Hamilton. Fewer than fifty detainees remained, but the major had talked about the early days when spy fever had prompted thousands of arrests and the facility was filled to capacity.

Most intriguing was the discussion about the tribunals conducted on a regular basis during which time a prisoner was given a hearing to determine whether he should remain interned. What would have changed to allow his release? Did the government continue to do background checks to determine the validity of the charges? How would they prove whether a man was a spy or not? Before the interview, he'd not given thought to the administrative aspect of handling the war.

He shuddered. When had man become so clinical about war? Perhaps the military had always been that way, and he'd been blessedly ignorant about the process.

The railroad car trundled over an uneven section of track, and Cora bumped into his shoulder. Her warmth permeated his sleeve, sending tingles down his arm. Did she feel that too?

"Sorry." He shifted away from her, hoping the distance would reduce his attraction to the beautiful reporter. It didn't.

"Sorry." She frowned and moved closer to the window. "Am I crowding you?"

"No, but I'm ready to be off this behemoth."

"Is it train travel in general or this particular trip? You've been pensive since shortly after we boarded."

"A lot on my mind, I guess."

"Anything you want to discuss?"

He tried to cross his long legs then gave up when his knee hit the seat in front of him. Pain shot up his thigh, and he sighed. Obviously, the engineer who'd designed the seating wasn't very tall.

"Van, do you want to get off at the next stop and walk around for a bit?" Concern lined her face. "Maybe grab something to eat before taking the next train?"

"Tempting, but I'd like to reach London sooner rather than later." He fidgeted, and his leg pressed against Cora's. He drew back as if burned. "I know I'm acting like a mountain lion with an injured paw. How about if we pick a topic totally unassociated with the war?"

A smile lit up her face, and she nodded.

The tightness in his chest eased. How could she make him feel better with a simple look? No one he'd ever dated could lighten his mood like Cora. He needed to remember she was just a colleague.

"Tell me more about Iowa. What did you like best about living there?"

Visions filled his mind's eye with fields of corn stretching to the horizon. His grandfather and him side by side in the endless rows picking ears. Back-breaking work, but satisfying. Smart enough to diversify his crops, Grandpop also grew oats.

A sharp jab to his ribs brought him back to the present.

Cora grinned. "You traveled back there, didn't you?"

His face warmed, and he nodded. "I miss the wide-open spaces and fresh air. I've smelled enough coal dust for a lifetime."

She giggled. "Me, too. Tell me what you were thinking about."

"I was remembering harvest time. Grandpop and I picking acres of corn. The horses hitched to the wagon, their harnesses jingling, their musky aroma mixing with the scent of dirt. Sun beating down on our backs, and every now and then a breeze would waft through, and the stalks would dance and wave."

"If you love farming so much, why did you go into newspaper work?"

"Grandpop was adamant that I make a living with my mind. He knows how tenuous farming life can be. One bad season of drought or insects, and a man can lose his property. He wanted a different path for me."

"But now you're over here in harm's way."

"Yeah, he wasn't crazy about that when I told him, but he understood my desire to do something bigger." His heart tugged. Would he make it home to see his grandfather again? "Enough about me. I know about Honolulu, but tell me about your journey to England. Not every gal gets this chance."

"Which is why I don't take my job for granted. My college roommate tried to get certified, but wasn't able to. She cobbled together a collection of small newspapers willing to take her stories then came over here on her own dime."

"Impressive."

"Yes, but she's not with an agency which doesn't give her credibility with some people." She sighed. "My certification took weeks. I think the government was looking for reasons not to appoint me, but my background check came back clean. This set of articles has been my first assignment since arriving. I wish I'd thought to apply when I got home from Pearl, but I was in a fog for months. Now, the war is drawing to a close. Not in the next few months, but maybe another year or eighteen months."

"In many ways, that year will feel like a lifetime." And then he'd never see her again. His heart fell at the thought.

"These few weeks certainly have felt that way."

"Then we'll get back to normal, whatever that means."

"It means the boys will come home, and we gals will be relegated to covering garden parties again." She frowned. "The real jobs will be few and far between."

"Surely, magazines like *Vogue* or *Collier's* will hire women. Consider your…uh…Miss O'Malley. I don't suppose she'd help you get on there."

Cora's laugh was harsh. "Hardly. And I wouldn't help her either."

"I may be out of line here, but you need to shed your anger and bitterness toward her—"

"You are out of line." Her face darkened. "My feud with Myrtle is none of your business."

"When the dispute impacts our work, it is my business." He took her hand in his, trying to ignore the way her palm nestled perfectly in his. "Those emotions aren't doing either one of you any good. What happened was a long time ago. Neither of you are the same person as you were then, but like you, she's seeking credibility in her career."

Cora snatched away her hand. "She's nothing like me, and if you paid attention, you'd know that."

Van crossed his arms. Why did he bother trying to understand women, especially Cora? She'd been a prickly pear since arriving at

Broadcasting House and wore a chip on her shoulder the size of an Iowa cornfield. Only two more articles remained in their assignment, then they could go their separate ways. And good riddance, too. He'd have more success wrestling a bobcat than figuring out what made Cora tick.

Chapter Fourteen

Seated across from Van at a table in Broadcasting House, Cora struggled to keep her mind on the notes she'd made for their article. She'd read the same sentence three times, and her brain refused to process the words. She stole a glance at him from under her bangs. He seemed intent on his work and oblivious to her agitation. Maybe he was a better actor than her.

Or maybe he *was* still upset with her emotional outburst this afternoon. He had every right to be irritated, even angry at her. Why couldn't she keep a rein on her temper? She'd let her past hurts surface, and they continued to churn and infiltrate her thoughts and behaviors. Why couldn't she let them go?

Instead, every time she saw Myrtle, insecurities and doubt surged, making her lash out and say stupid things. Van must be ready to sever their partnership, and she didn't blame him.

She wiped her damp palms on her skirt then patted her hair. "Van?" Her voice cracked, and she cleared her throat. "Van, sorry to interrupt, but I wanted to say something."

He laid down his pencil and looked up, eyes shuttered and guarded. "Yes?"

"I'm sorry for overreacting earlier. I can go into a long-winded explanation, but that would sound like excuses and justification for my behavior. I was terribly rude, and I hope you can find it in your heart to forgive me at some point." She shrugged, and her face heated. "I'm dragging around a lot of uncertainty, and it gushes out at the worst possible moments, spilling on everyone around me. Anyway, I'm sorry. I don't know what else to say."

Van blew out a breath and ran his fingers through his hair, then leaned his elbows on the table. "Apology accepted, although I must admit your vehemence took me by surprise." He cradled her hand in his.

A jolt of electricity shot through her palm. Did he feel that, too? The imperceptible widening of his eyes seemed to say he did. She could not allow her attraction to get in the way of her job. Too many women gave up opportunities to stay home and have babies. She wouldn't be one of them.

His thumb drew circles on the back of her hand. His lips were moving, but she could hardly focus on what he was saying. She blinked and forced herself to listen.

"As you indicated, your life isn't any of my business, but your reaction tells me there's more to this story than meets the eye. Yes, Miss O'Malley is annoying and trying to scoop you. Every other reporter out there is doing the same thing. And she hurt you, too, but you admitted her stealing whatshisname…"

"Louis."

"Louis…wasn't as bad as you initially felt because of meeting your husband. If you need to talk about what's really bothering you, I'm a good listener." He smirked. "Well, not always, but I promise to be this time." He leaned forward and tipped up her chin so she could meet his eyes. "You're a good writer. Your stories inform, yet at the same time, touch an emotional chord with readers, making them invest themselves in the topic, or more importantly, the people you're writing about. And you may not want to hear it, but you're a beautiful woman, on the inside and the outside. Your faith…well, I wish mine was as strong."

She gaped at him, her eyes wide. He thought she had a strong faith. Little did he know about the tenuous hold she had trusting God to work out His plan in her life. She was a mess, a bundle of anxiety and indecision, second-guessing every choice she'd ever made.

A giggle bubbled up inside then spilled over, becoming a chuckle, then finally a fully formed laugh. Ridiculous. His comment was absolutely ridiculous. A child had more faith than her. Her amusement turned to sadness and regret, the emotions fighting for supremacy. Her stomach clenched, and breakfast threatened to appear. Tears sprang to her eyes, and she blinked them away. But the moisture welled up and soon overflowed down her cheeks.

Van's expression told her everything she needed to know. He was disappointed, disgusted, and disdainful. One more person judging her, and if she looked around the room, she'd probably see the rest of the men with the same opinion.

Swiping at her face, Cora shoved back the chair and stood. "I'm sorry. I should go." She snatched her pocketbook and papers from the table.

He leapt up, his chair screeching against the wooden floor. He grabbed her arm. "Wait. Please wait."

She studied him through her swimming vision. Why did he want her to stay? He had to be embarrassed about the scene she was making.

With a fluid motion, he released her, donned his jacket, then collected his pages, before taking her items and adding them to the stack. He wrapped his arm around her shoulder and led her out the door. "I think some sunshine is in order, don't you?"

Lips trembling, she nodded. By now he must think her a complete ninny, but he was being so nice, she couldn't bring herself to run from his care.

They made their way to a bench. He lowered her onto the seat, then pulled a handkerchief from his pocket and handed it to her. "Guess I should have done that first." He squatted in front of her, concern darkening his eyes.

She mopped the wetness from her face and attempted a smile that probably ended up as a grimace. Her chest tight, she took a deep breath. She must look a fright. "Thank you. I'm not sure what came over me." Her voice was scratchy and broken.

"Hmmm. Worry, homesickness, stress." He cocked his head and grinned. "Need I go on?"

"Why are you being such a gentleman? I've been nothing but beastly."

"Like I said, there seems to be more happening than you're letting on." He cupped his ears. "I'm ready to listen, when you're ready to talk."

Exhaling, she patted the bench. "I'd rather you weren't staring at me the entire time."

"Fair enough." He rose and tucked a stray lock of hair behind her ear before dropping beside her.

She quivered at his touch. Clutching the soggy hanky, she sat, eyes downcast. "I've already told you that my marriage feels distant and surreal because of the lack of time we had together, but the truth is I'm not sure our relationship would have deepened even if he came home."

Her face heated, and she continued to avoid his eyes. "Sure, we exchanged letters, but Brian couldn't tell me what he was doing, and I never seemed to have much to say in return. Our correspondence became a study in weather and inanities. I can barely remember the sound of his voice. For some reason, seeing Myrtle resurrects my guilt, and well…you see how I react." She swallowed the lump in her throat. "I'm a shallow, terrible person, and my faith is hanging on by a thread."

He stroked her back, and shivers galloped up her spine.

"Sounds like you have an honest faith. God can handle your doubts. In fact, I think He welcomes them because you're being real. Too many times, we withhold how we really feel, thinking that it's a sin to question Him or tell him we're upset, even angry."

With an audible sigh, Van rubbed his forehead. "Now, I can't tell you what to think about your marriage, and all the woulda-coulda-shoulda thoughts that assail you, but I know if you hand them off to God, He'll wrap His arms around you and soften the pain, maybe even make you feel some sense of joy about the time you had with your husband. Mind you, the change won't happen overnight and will take a lot of prayer, but He will heal you."

"When did you get to be so wise?" She looked at him through tear-filled eyes.

A sheepish grin quirked his lips. "I won't bore you with the details, but doubt and I are old friends."

The constriction in her muscles eased. Why had she thought him so awful? He'd dropped everything to comfort and console her, acting the part of a true friend. She shouldn't get too used to his kindness. They'd be going their separate ways after their assignment was complete. Two more articles, and they'd be done. Too soon.

Chapter Fifteen

"Thanks, Van, for your honesty and compassion." Cora's face heated. Why did she have to blush at the slightest bit of awkwardness? "I'm embarrassed to have had a breakdown. Behaviors like this prompt guys to think we women can't handle a difficult situation, that we're too emotional."

"Maybe the *other* guys." He winked and thumped his chest. "I'm much more progressive. If I was a betting man, I'd wager the men suffer from anxiety, perhaps hiding their feelings behind bravado. Are you well enough to return upstairs, or would you rather take a walk or pick this up again tomorrow?"

"The weather is delightful. How about if we stay outside?" She frowned. "Unless the noise is too much of a distraction."

"Pfft. Pedestrians and light traffic are nothing compared to the chaos that crowds of reporters produce. Working from here is great." He leaned back on the bench and pulled out their papers. Sifting through the pages, he handed her part of the stack. "I think these are yours."

"Thanks." Cora took a deep breath. He remained gracious, but had donned his professional journalist's persona, putting her emotional outburst behind them. She studied her notes, trying to ignore the close proximity of his warm frame. Built nothing like any man she'd ever dated, Van towered over her with broad shoulders and raven-black hair. She had to look way up to gaze into his crystal-blue eyes. Brian had been wiry and blond as had Louis. Neither had been much taller than her own five-foot-three. Her high school dates were a distant memory, but they seemed scrawny in contrast to her partner.

"I think that's the best way to approach the article. What do you think?"

Uh-oh. She'd managed to miss every word he'd said with her ruminations. Could she fake her way through the conversation? "That sounds good to me."

He narrowed his eyes. "Exactly which part?"

She huffed out a breath. "All right. I confess. I didn't hear you. I was…uh…still caught up in the previous conversation. I'm okay now." Good grief, Cora, keep your mind in the game and off the features of your handsome partner. She straightened the papers and gripped her pencil. "Ready."

Concern darkened his eyes. "Are you sure? Because we've got several days before the deadline and can take a break."

"No, I'd rather put together a rough outline, if possible."

"Great." He crossed his legs and tossed out several ideas about how to start the piece.

They worked for over an hour honing the objective of the article then organizing their research. The sun dipped behind the surrounding buildings, and a light breeze ruffled their pages.

Cora shivered and pulled her jacket closer. The day had begun unusually warm, and she'd chosen a lighter coat than normal, a choice she now regretted.

Van glanced over then stood and shed his sport coat. He placed it around her shoulders. "Better?"

The scent of his aftershave clung to the material, and she stifled the urge to draw the coat closer to her nose. "Yes, but won't you be cold?"

"Nah, these temperatures are nothing like what we have in Iowa on an autumn or winter day." He flexed his muscles and grinned. "I can handle a slight chill."

She giggled. "A regular Superman."

"Exactly. I champion truth, justice, and the American way." He chuckled. "Although he's from Kansas, and I'm from Iowa."

"No doubt a very important distinction."

A smile continued to tug at his lips. "No doubt."

He pulled out his pocket watch and flipped it open. "We've made excellent progress. It's nearly four o'clock. Too early for high tea." He affected an exaggerated British accent. "But I'm starving."

"I've never been one to stand on ceremony." She snickered and mimicked his pronunciation. "Low tea, it is."

"There's no such thing as…oh…funny." His eyes twinkled as he rose then bowed and gave her his papers. "Would you be so kind as to tuck our pages in your pocketbook? I seem to have left my satchel at home."

With a nod, she stuffed their work into her handbag.

Hand on the small of her back, Van guided her away from Broadcasting House.

Despite her blouse and two jackets, the warmth of his palm sent goose bumps dancing up her spine. She swallowed a gasp and tightened the grip on her purse.

"Well, isn't this cozy?"

Cora's head whipped around at the voice she'd recognize anywhere.

Myrtle stood at the intersection, eyebrows lifted high on her forehead. Dressed as if she had an appointment with King George, she wore a blue silk suit and matching pumps. White gloves covered her hands. "You two sure look chummy. I didn't realize you were an item." She shook her pointer finger at Van. "You've been holding out on me, Mr. Toppel."

Van dipped his head. "Miss O'Malley."

"Cora, darling, are you sure you want to get involved during wartime? And with a coworker? Tsk, tsk. Not very appropriate. Wouldn't you agree?"

Cora opened her mouth to reply, but Van responded before she could say anything.

"Not sure that our relationship, whatever it is, is any of your business, Miss O'Malley. We're grown-ups and professionals."

Her eyebrows disappeared into her hairline. "Aren't you the coy one? I'm simply looking out for your best interests. Workplace romances are frowned upon by the higher-ups."

"Thanks for the advice, but we don't need it." Van pressed his hand against Cora's back.

The tension in her shoulders seeped away. If she was reading his gesture correctly, he was telling her not to worry. Protecting and comforting her again.

"So, you are just friends?"

Moisture sprang out on Cora's palms. Surely, he would confirm that and nothing more.

"Would you find it so hard to believe if Cora and I were seeing each other, Miss O'Malley?"

Myrtle sniffed and looked down her nose. "Yes. She's nice enough, but she's nothing like the woman a man like you should be seeing."

Cora pressed her lips together and wondered at the urge she had to push Myrtle onto the sidewalk, mess up her outfit, and wipe the smirk off the woman's face. Her conscience pricked her, and she sighed. *Forgive me, Lord. I'm letting my emotions get in the way again.*

Van draped his arm around Cora's shoulders.

She startled, but didn't move from under his embrace.

"Look, Miss O'Malley. This discussion is going nowhere. You know nothing about me and what I am looking for in a girlfriend. Cora is bright and beautiful. Her faith makes her even more attractive. I'm quite happy with our relationship, so I suggest you keep your advice to yourself."

Cora's heart banged inside her chest. He said she was pretty…no…beautiful. Were his words for show or did he mean them? He'd insinuated they were dating. How soon before that rumor raced through the ranks? Was Myrtle right? Would there be ramifications to his claim?

Chapter Sixteen

Arm still wrapped around Cora's shoulder, Van led her down the sidewalk. "Are you up for a stroll? I thought we could look at the flowers in Regent's Park. The roses won't be open in Queen Mary's Garden, but there must be something blooming."

Face flushed, Cora nodded. "Perfect. I'd appreciate looking at something other than rubble and boarded-up windows. I don't suppose we could work an article about our visit."

He hugged her to him for a brief moment. "Always thinking, aren't you? Maybe something about pursuing normalcy during times of difficulty." He shrugged. "Let me give it some thought. If nothing else, we'll have a delightful evening."

Her pink cheeks deepened to red, and she nodded, then slipped out from his hold.

His heart fell. Cora fit perfectly in his embrace.

They ambled north on Portland Place, silent except for the sound of their feet crunching on the ever-present dust. Few shops were open, and those that were had little merchandise to offer. The windows not covered in sheets of wood were crisscrossed with tape, lending a Tudor flavor to the buildings.

The tantalizing aroma of baking bread wafted toward them. Van's stomach rumbled, and he pointed to an open door under a sign that swung in the breeze: Bea's Breads. "I vote we stop in here."

Cora rushed forward. "Me, too." She lifted her chin and sniffed. "And I detect potato soup, too."

"Quite the investigative reporter."

She giggled, and they entered the bakery.

A petite, redheaded woman hunched over a table kneading a large lump of dough. Two young girls sat at one of the tables drawing pictures. They looked up and gawked at Van and Cora. "Mum?"

The woman turned, a smudge of flour on one cheek beneath twinkling green eyes. "I'm Bea. Welcome to my shop. I hope yer hungry. Several loaves of bread just came out of the oven, and the soup should be finished cooking."

"We're starving." Cora grabbed Van's hand and dragged him toward the counter. "We could smell your delicious food outside." She gestured toward the children. "Yours? They're cute as buttons."

Bea nodded, her smile wide. "Nancy's seven and Joan is eight." Her smile dimmed as she cut generous slices from a steaming loaf. "Their school closed two years ago, so they spend most days with me. We work on their numbers, letters, and reading during the morning hours, and in the afternoons they color or play games. 'Tis tough to be a little one these days…so much sadness. I do what I can to keep them cheery."

"You're a good mother." Van laid some coins on the counter. "Their father…?"

"Best I can tell in Italy somewhere, making his way up the boot. I still get mail, and he referred to a fountain we visited on our honeymoon…not by name, of course."

Clasping her hands to her heart, Cora said, "I'm glad he's still alive. I'll pray for his continued safety."

"That's nice of you. I've also been prayin' that the good Lord sees fit to bring him home. It's been hard enough on the girls having him away, but to lose him…" Bea sniffled as she ladled a generous portion of soup into a pair of bowls, then set them on the counter along with a plate filled with bread slices. "Eat up. There's more if you want it."

Van picked up the dishes and carried them to one of the tables. "This will be plenty."

Cora stopped next to the girls. "Didn't you do a wonderful job on your pictures? You're both very talented."

The youngsters beamed and looked at their mom who mouthed, "Say thank you."

"Thank you!" Nancy and Joan spoke in unison, their words shy and uncertain.

"You're welcome, ladies."

They tittered, and Van smiled. He'd thought it once before, but her graciousness on the heels of her emotional upset with Myrtle told him she'd make a great mother someday. She deserved the chance.

Van dipped his bread into the creamy-looking concoction then took a bite. His eyes widened. Who knew potatoes could taste so good? He tried not to wolf down the food but was unsuccessful. Minutes later, his bowl was empty, and only two pieces of bread remained.

The bowl in front of Cora was also empty, and she wiped her mouth with a napkin. "That was one of the best meals I've had in ages."

"Agreed." He grinned. "If she wasn't already married…"

"Yeah, right." She snorted a laugh. "As if you were the marrying kind."

He grunted and pressed his hands to his chest as if he'd been stabbed. "That's not a nice thing to say, Miss Strealer. Especially after I told Miss O'Malley about our *relationship.*"

Shadows passed across her face, then she sent him a saucy smile. "Sure, but we're only dating, remember? It's not as if you proposed or anything."

His jaw dropped, and his belly buzzed as if a flock of hummingbirds had taken flight. The sharp intake of breath from Bea was audible, and he cringed at what she might think about their conversation. Did the proprietress expect him to take the opportunity to drop on one knee and pop the question? How would Cora respond if he did?

Whoa. Where did that thought come from? Granted, she was beginning to mean something to him, but as a wife? No, and definitely not in wartime.

He took a deep breath and hoped she wouldn't be offended if he played along with her flippancy. "True, and don't be looking for one any time soon."

She threw back her head and laughed. "What a relief." Tossing her napkin on the table, she stood. A smirk tugged at her mouth, and she held out her hand. "I'm ready for a turn around the park."

"A perfect way to walk off our meal." Van laced his fingers with hers and nodded to Bea who stared at them, mouth in a perfect O.

Cora waved with her other hand at the trio. "Goodbye and thank you. Bea, your food was absolutely delicious. We'll be back, I'm sure."

Van led her out the door, and they continued their walk toward the park. A breeze lifted Cora's hair, and he caught the floral scent of her shampoo. How did she remain so fresh and clean tramping London's dirty streets?

They crossed Park Crescent and entered Park Square Garden, the ground soft beneath their feet. A few minutes later they turned onto Outer Circle headed for York Bridge. Somewhere in the distance a church bell tolled the hour. Five o'clock already. Time spent with Cora flew on eagle's wings.

He pulled her along and smiled when she skipped to keep up with his long legs. Slowing his pace, he said, "I'm sorry. I forgot about your stubby little legs."

She yanked her hand out of his and stuck out her tongue. "I'll show you stubby little legs." With a shout, she ran along the path, her Victory rolls tumbling from their pins. The sun shimmered on her corn silk-colored tresses, and her skirts fluttered with every step.

His mouth dried at the vision of her trim figure racing away. He blinked. Away. She was getting away. He sprinted after her, legs pumping to catch up. She pivoted and waved, her face dazzling with joy, then continued running. Minute by minute, she was burrowing her way into his heart.

Cora lagged, her breath loud and ragged.

Van drew alongside her. "Speed, but no stamina, Strealer. Too bad. You almost won." He put two fingers to his forehead in mock salute and dashed past her to the entrance of the Inner Circle that surrounded Queen Mary's Garden. He jogged in place and raised his arms. "The winner and grand champeeeen, Van Toppel. Woohoo!"

Seconds later, she crossed the finish line, her face aglow. "Congratulations, but you know I let you win, right?"

"Nice try, honey. You lost fair and square." He shadowboxed. "No one can beat me when I set my mind to winning."

"Uh huh. Whatever you say, Superman. Or is it Clark Kent?"

"Ha! Show a little respect to your elders."

"Only if my elder deserves it." She danced away then beckoned. "Come on, let's check out the Japanese Garden Island. One of the girls at my boardinghouse visited a few days ago and said it's exquisite." She sobered up. "Wait. Does it feel weird to be at war with Japan yet sightseeing one of their gardens? Perhaps we should look at something else."

"What did you have in mind?"

She shrugged. "How about the little lake farther up the path? That might be fun."

He bowed. "Your wish is my command." Any activity with this sparkling woman would be enjoyable. Something told him life in the future wouldn't be nearly as bright or as fun without her. But she might reject him once she discovered his secret.

Chapter Seventeen

Shadows lengthened as Cora glanced at Van. He'd grown pensive in the last few minutes, and she hesitated to intrude on his thoughts. Unless, of course, he needed cheering up. How was she to know what to do?

She stopped along the shoreline of the Y-shaped pond on the west side of the park and bent to pick up a stone. She'd spent many hours with her sisters skipping rocks on the lakes at home. A gust of wind tangled her hair around her face, and she scraped away the errant locks. The aroma of grass, water, and vegetation pushed the ever-present smell of coal to the background. She took a deep breath and heaved the stone toward the water.

One—two—three—four skips, then a plop as the rock sunk.

"Not bad for a girl." The clouds in Van's eyes had cleared, and he tossed a stone from hand to hand. "Care to make a wager that I can't beat you?"

"Not worth my time." Cora crossed her arms and looked off in the distance, pretending to be unaffected by his dare.

"Afraid you'll lose again?" He moved directly in front of her and turned her chin so she had to look in his eyes.

Those startling deep, expressive eyes. Her stomach tightened. "Oh, all right. Go ahead and pitch the thing, proving once and for all that you're Superman."

Van swung his arm, hurling the rock toward the water.

One—two—three. Plunk.

Cora mimicked Van's early victory dance by jogging in place, hands raised over her head. "What were you saying about my skills as a girl? And don't you dare claim you let me win."

His face flushed, and he chuckled. "Yes, ma'am." He raked his fingers through his hair and sighed. "Hard to believe there's a war on with a day like today. Beautiful weather. Lovely scenery. Time away from chasing stories."

She nodded and gestured to a wooden bench nestled under a small tree.

They sat in silence for several minutes.

Cora licked her lips. "Life never quite turns out how you plan, does it? I mean, not always in a bad way, but we humans think we can arrange every moment, and honestly, we can't. A ludicrous assumption on our part."

"You've got that right. And like you said, sometimes it's positive, but I certainly never expected my career to take me overseas to a war zone. I've had a chance to make history with some of my coverage and meet some of my heroes." He gazed at her for a long moment. "And make new friends."

Her heart thumped. "I'm certainly a different person than when I got here. My experiences have changed the way I look at…people, government, leadership, sacrifice, my job…everything."

He laced his fingers and cradled his knee. "Nothing will ever be the same again. People will talk about life before the war and after. This conflict has already outpaced the Great War in terms of money spent and lives lost."

"We're a maudlin pair, aren't we?" She rubbed her finger along the seam of her skirt. "Some good has come from the evil. You're from Iowa, and I'm from New Hampshire. Our paths never would have crossed if it wasn't for the war."

"A most serendipitous fortune, my dear." He grinned, then his smile faltered. "Listen, if we're going to be friends and not just colleagues, there's something I need to tell you. I-I-I hope it doesn't change our new camaraderie."

What could be so awful that he thought she'd shun him? Had he broken the law? Done jail time for refusing to name a source? Was divorced? Her mouth dried, and she swallowed heavily.

She laid her hand on his arm. "Friends through thick and thin." Would she regret the promise?

"I…uh…I'm German."

"What?" Cora drew back. "I thought you were an American. How did you get accredited?" Her thoughts hearkened back to their conversations while working on the internment article. He *had* been hiding something.

Van held up his hands in surrender. "I am a U.S. citizen, but I have German heritage. My great-great grandfather came to America from Darmstadt in 1806."

She flopped against the bench. "Oh, well, surely that's no big deal. The feds would have unearthed that during your background check. Not that their opinion matters to me, but they don't seem to mind, and I don't either."

"Really?" His face lit up, and he grabbed her hands. "That means a lot to me."

Her fingers trembled under his. She had to keep in mind he was just a friend. Why couldn't she get her body to remember that? "You're a good, kind, and decent man. Just because some family members emigrated from Germany nearly a hundred and fifty years ago, doesn't make you a Nazi or a spy. Anyone who thinks it should have his or her head examined."

"Did you read our article on the internment camps? Or the ones at home?"

"Fortunately, both governments have come to their senses and released most of the people they should. But in the beginning, hysteria won out over good judgment."

"Thank you for believing in me."

She winked. "You'll just owe me one." What was she doing? Since when was she a flirty kind of girl? Her face warmed, and she hoped her cheeks weren't blazing. She cleared her throat. "Besides, evil is rarely tied to a particular ethnic group. We've all sinned and fallen short. No one has the corner on the market for heinous behaviors and beliefs."

"Well said."

The sun dipped behind the trees, and the breeze that brushed her cheeks sent icy fingers along her spine. She shivered. Why hadn't she brought a warmer jacket? He'd think her foolish, unprepared.

"You're cold. Shame on me. I shouldn't have kept you out this late." He rose, shed his jacket, and draped it over her shoulders.

"Thank you, but now you'll be chilled."

"I'll be fine." He dropped onto the bench.

The seat's legs creaked, then one pair cracked and gave way, snapping in half.

Cora tumbled against Van who rolled onto the ground with a grunt. She landed in a heap on top of him. Her face was inches from his, and her heart beat like a timpani in a Beethoven symphony.

Before she could scramble away, he wrapped his arms around her. His pupils dilated, turning his cobalt-blue eyes into liquid ink. Her breath hitched as his gaze seemed to caress her face.

He lifted his head, and his lips brushed hers. Gently, tenderly. Then his embrace tightened, and he pressed his mouth on hers, saying what words could not. She returned his kiss and wondered at feelings that swept over her. Was it possible that she'd found love a second time?

Chapter Eighteen

The raucous screech of a magpie split the air, startling Van. He broke the kiss, and his arms sprang apart. What had he done? He licked his lips, Cora's sweet taste lingering on his mouth.

Cora's eyes flew open, and she stared at him for a long moment before rolling off his chest onto her knees. Pink to the roots of her golden-blonde hair, she ducked her head and struggled to rise.

He climbed to his feet then bent and helped her stand. Would she slap him as he deserved for taking liberties? He hadn't meant to kiss her, but the glow in her gaze combined with the proximity of her soft-looking lips overrode his common sense. He'd taken advantage of her closeness and probably ruined any chance of continuing their tenuous friendship.

Still avoiding his eyes, she brushed dirt and grass from her clothes.

Clearing his throat, he bent and picked up his fedora that had flown from his head during the fall. "I'm sorry. You have every right to be upset. I don't know what came over me. It won't happen again. Please forgive me. I don't want to lose our relationship…friendship. I plead insanity, and you can't very well blame a crazy person, can you?"

A snicker, then a chuckle. She lifted her head and nodded. "With all that rambling, you're proving your case of madness. All is forgiven, but I'll probably remind you about the incident at inopportune moments to keep you on your toes."

"As you should, but I'm not looking forward to them."

"Excellent." Her eyes danced, and she smirked. "Gotta stay ahead of you."

"Now that I'm back in your good graces, what do you think we should do about the bench? Where should we report the damage? I hate to leave it crumpled."

"I don't suppose there's a Broken Bench Department. The countless number of bureaucratic agencies is mind-boggling."

Van snorted a laugh at her impish expression. "Good thought, but I doubt it."

He checked his watch in the waning light. "It's getting late. The Air Raid Precaution wardens will be patrolling soon and wonder while we're still out and about with no destination in mind. Let's leave the bench till morning then see if one of the secretaries knows how to take care of the situation."

"Brilliant. Those gals have solved more than one touchy problem for me."

"Really? Care to share?"

"Nope." She slung her pocketbook strap over her shoulder. "Despite you unceremoniously pitching me onto the ground, I've had a lovely time. We got off to a rocky start, but I now I can't imagine reporting the war with anyone else."

His chest swelled, and he mentally rolled his eyes at his schoolboy reaction. "Same here, but no need to say goodbye. I'm going to walk you to your boardinghouse. Darkness will be full-on before you get home. I'd feel better if you had an escort."

"So my safety is all about how you feel, and not my actual security." Hands on hips, she stood with her head cocked, a mock frown creasing her forehead.

"Something like that."

Cora burst out laughing, and he joined her, the earlier awkwardness dissipating. She was a good sport. He'd nearly blown it, but their kiss obviously didn't mean anything to her, so she was able to cast the moment aside. Was he relieved or disappointed?

"Get a move on, folks. The park is closing." A stooped man wearing a tin hat and ARP band around his upper arm, approached. "And have a care. It's a new moon tonight, meaning pitch darkness after the sun finishes setting."

"Yes, sir." Van held out his arm, crooked at the elbow. The man's words gave him an excuse to tuck Cora close to his side. She didn't need to know the real reason.

She slipped her fingers into the bend of his arm, and he patted her hand. "Shall we away, Miss Strealer."

"I can find my way home on my own, Van, although I appreciate your offer."

"I don't mind escorting you. Like the man said, it's going to be difficult to see." He frowned. After their frivolity, why was she turning down his offer?

"Yes, but I'll be fine. There were few streetlamps in New Hampshire. I made my own way home on plenty of inky-black nights. London is no different."

"Not to intrude, miss, but I'd say the number of ruffians in our fair city is higher than that in your rural state."

Her head whipped around toward the warden. "What do you know of my home?"

"My sister lives in Maine, and I was fortunate to visit her many years ago before the war. We took a trip to the White Mountains. The scenery was beautiful, but remote."

Cora squeezed Van's arm. "Did you hear that? He's been to America, to New Hampshire." She leaned toward the man. "I wish we could stay and reminisce, but you have a job to do. My heart is a little lighter for having met you, sir."

The warden executed a deep bow. "Glad to have brightened your evening, miss." He touched his helmet. "G'night."

Van waved with his free hand. "I agree with our new friend about the *ruffians*. Please let me walk you home."

A deep sigh sounded. "Okay, but I don't have to like it…well, not the actual walk, but the fact I need a man with me. Frustrating, you know?"

"Yes, tough to feel invincible when you have to fear for your safety from unscrupulous men." He let sarcasm coat his words.

She slapped his shoulder and chortled. "Exactly. At least you understand." Another sigh. "But the fact of the matter is eventually you're not going to be there, to keep me safe, to take care of me. Whether it's after the war or the end of this assignment. Don't you see? I can only lean on myself. What we insinuated to Myrtle isn't true. We aren't romantically involved, so time will move on, and we will too."

His breath hitched, and a rock settled in his stomach. Cora was right. Even if they remained friends, sooner or later, they'd go their separate ways. The future suddenly looked bleaker.

Chapter Nineteen

The morning sun seeped through the clouds but failed to warm the misty air. Cora pulled her jacket tighter around her frame and sped up. By the time she arrived at Broadcasting House, her cheeks and hands tingled from the chilly breeze. She shivered as she yanked open the door and hurried inside.

Would Van be upstairs?

Cora pressed her fingers to her lips, remembering the feel of his mouth on hers. Soft, yet firm. She'd lost herself in the moment, Brian a distant memory. As a widow, she certainly wasn't innocent in the ways of men and women, but somehow her relationship with Van felt young and fresh and…exciting. If what they had could even be called a relationship.

What did they have?

She'd played along when he seemed distraught over what he deemed to be a mistake. His embarrassment was palpable, and he apologized six ways from Sunday as her sister Emily would say. She didn't want to embarrass him further by letting on that the kiss had affected her.

Conversation filled the entryway as she headed toward the stairs. More time to think about what happened than if she rode the elevator. She gripped the railing and trudged up the steps.

Only weeks ago, Van's presence set her teeth on edge. He'd been arrogant and condescending. And then he wasn't. He'd apologized. Again. And again. Slowly, his behavior changed to one of acceptance then friendship. His teasing was brotherly, almost as if they were schoolkids, and he was dipping her pigtails in the inkwell.

His intelligence was alluring. He challenged her with his questions and ideas, making her think hard to come up with answers and rebuttals. She relished the opportunities to spar with the handsome reporter.

Brian had been good looking, but Van was movie-star gorgeous. Standing just over six feet, his broad shoulders made him seem taller. He walked with assurance, and his dark-blue eyes missed nothing. He should have been a detective. Criminals would give up as soon as they saw him coming.

Cora chuckled to herself as her imagination ran away with itself. Since when did she act the part of the simpering fan? Was her behavior a result of being far from family in a foreign country where no one knew her? She could do or be whatever she wanted to be. Totally reinvent herself. Had she already transformed herself?

Maybe the war was changing her. She certainly wasn't the first woman to be impacted by the conflict. She shook her head. The war was blamed for everything, good and bad. Sure, she was different. Brian's death. Moving back home. Taking the job overseas. Meeting Van.

Her palms moistened. Her thoughts had come full circle.

"Don't be daft, girl. Get a move on. You've got work to do." She hurried up the stairs, the soles of her shoes slapped against the treads. "Enough introspection. One kiss. No big deal."

She pushed open the door, her breath coming in ragged bursts. "A little more exercise would do you well. Winded after three flights. For shame."

"Talking to yourself, Strealer? That doesn't bode well." Van's voice brought her up short.

Heart thudding in her chest, she pinned a smile on her face and turned. The resident hummingbirds had taken flight in her stomach, so she pressed her hand against her middle to quiet the buzz. No good. The pesky birds continue to fly. So much for no big deal, but she could act the sophisticate. She had to. "Hey, I'm the smartest person I know."

His head tipped back, and he laughed. Long and hard.

Drawn in by his response, her smile widened into genuine amusement, then she giggled. Then joined him in laughter.

The other reporters stared at them, some in confusion, others in obvious delight.

Van's laughter finally slowed then ceased altogether. He mopped his eyes with his handkerchief then returned the hanky to his pocket. A grin still on his lips, he said, "I do admire your pluck, young lady. And you're right. You are the smartest person you know, me included."

Cora ducked her head. She might try to play the worldly wise woman, and maybe she wasn't a total yokel, but deep down, she was a small-town girl at heart. Community events, family dinners, and school football games were her cup of tea. She had never learned how to handle the machinations of others, which is probably why she fell prey to Myrtle's deception.

Could she trust Van not to trifle with her heart? Thus far, he'd proven himself trustworthy, but her sweating palms and skittering pulse combined with the memory of their kiss challenged her ability to think when he was around. To discern what he was about.

"Are you okay, Cora?" Concern creased Van's forehead. "You seem to be having an argument with yourself. Anything I can do?"

Her face warmed. Now, he'd really wonder about her sanity. "Yeah. Fine. Shouldn't we get started? We need to talk about possibilities for our next story."

His eyes shuttered, and he gestured to a small table in the corner, away from the typewriters. "Sure. We've already talked about a couple, but I've got some additional ideas."

She pulled her pocketbook close. Had he really expected her to share what she'd been thinking? He'd seen her at her worst. Perhaps she had nothing to lose. "Uh, I *was* bickering with myself. Embarrassed to be caught at it."

The clouds cleared from his gaze, and he chuckled. "Nothing to be ashamed of. I do it all the time." He pulled out a chair for her. "Okay, let the creativity begin."

Dropping into the seat, she pulled out her steno pad. "I jotted down some thoughts, too. Maybe we'll get more than one feasible story." She sent him a smug look. "As smart as we both are…"

He grinned.

Her heart flip-flopped. She might as well give up now. His kindness and gentle teasing, along with his steadfast faith and breathtaking good looks were like nothing she'd ever experienced. Even with Brian. Van had worked his way into her heart and would take a piece with him when they separated. She pressed her lips together to stem the trembling.

⸺ ••◦◉◦•• ⸺

Van settled in the chair next to Cora, the heady scent of her shampoo filling his nose. He blinked and spread his pages on the table. If he couldn't school his emotions, they'd never get anything done. She was alternately staid and sassy, and he enjoyed both sides of her personality. Whether he liked it or not, he was beginning to care a great deal about his spunky partner. Were his feelings as strong as he'd insinuated to Miss O'Malley?

He cleared his throat. Focus, man.

"Yes?" Cora looked up from her notes, eyes wide. "Did I miss something?"

"No. The cigarette smoke is…uh…getting to me. My throat is dry." He gestured to her pages. "Whatcha got?"

"I wrote down the ideas we mentioned while researching our other pieces: how crime has changed during wartime and the impact of schools being closed for lack of teachers. I also thought of exploring stories of neighbors helping neighbors during the war, in big ways and small. Sort of a home-front version of Ernie Pyle's columns."

"People like seeing their names in the paper. Now that the end of the war is in sight we could ask people what their plans are. Could be tricky depending on who we ask. Widows and parents who've lost their kids may not have considered the future."

Cora frowned and picked at the edge of the paper. "Most haven't. The focus is on getting through each day, one step at a time. An hour is as much future as some people can handle." Her eyes moistened, and she blinked rapidly. "For the first six months after Brian passed, rising and getting dressed were my only goals each day."

Her eyes took on the distant gaze of nostalgia. "My folks must have contacted my former boss because he showed up at the house one day and offered me a job. Pushed me into it, really. I turned him down, but he wouldn't take no for an answer. In fact, he came armed with an assignment." A dry laugh punctuated her words. "A four-hundred-word piece on the town manager's wedding. Not exactly Pulitzer Prize-winning material, but doing the article reminded me that I loved to write. Anyway, the piece must have been halfway decent because he gave me two more assignments, and I slowly crawled back into the land of the living."

Van touched the back of her hand. "I'm sure your work was much better than you're giving yourself credit for." He gave himself a mental slap. He'd brought up widows, ripping the bandage off her grief. How callous. She didn't seem offended that he'd reminded her of her loss, but he'd made her sad.

"Possibly." She shrugged. "Enough about me. What ideas did you bring?"

The look of dejection on her face clawed at his heart. "Women. We could do an entire series of articles on women. You've been a testament to the tenacity, strength, and perseverance of your gender. Until you came into my life, I hadn't given thought to what it would be like to live in a society that treated me like a second-class citizen. To have to push to be heard and valued. Yet since the beginning of this war, women have leapt into every nook and cranny to support the effort. And proven themselves every bit as capable as men."

With a dismissive wave, she shook her head. "How gallant of you to say, but to focus on only half the population doesn't make for good press. Besides, for generations men have been raised to provide and protect us. We can't expect that belief system to change overnight, or even in a handful of years. As men are exposed to our abilities, attitudes will change."

"But will you and I live to see it?" He leaned forward, inches from her face. "How long will women be stuck having to live with daddy or marry someone they don't love to be taken care of? Doesn't seem fair."

An errant strand of hair fell across her cheek, and she tucked it behind her ear while giving him a wry smile. "Since when is life fair?"

"Rarely." With a deep breath, he reached for her hand and cradled her warm palm in his. "You returned home, but wouldn't you rather marry again? Or will you try to make it on your own, you know, since you do have a career?"

For a long moment, neither of them said anything.

He repressed the urge to withdraw his hand. She didn't seem upset by his questions, but she hadn't responded either. His stomach clenched. How would she answer?

Finally, when he could stand it no longer, she looked up, mouth set in a slash. "Honestly? The thought of marrying again terrifies me. I barely remember what being married was like. We spent more time apart than together. I'm not convinced I have what it takes for a successful marriage."

"Why would you say that? You're intelligent, loving, and kind. You would be a wonderful wife. But what specifically scares you?"

Her mouth worked, but no words came out. She tried to pull away, but he clung to her hand. "Not so fast, *Strealer*. We've started down this road. Let's finish the journey. You're safe with me."

"I am, aren't I, *Toppel*?" Relief swept over her expression. "Okay, I know I'm young, and countless friends and relatives who meant well said I should find someone and settle down, but I wonder if I'm being disloyal to Brian. To his memory. He died in service to his country. Should I honor that?"

"By remaining single?" Van cocked his head. "I'm not following your logic."

"We would still be married if it weren't for the war, and he gave up our lives together so he could serve."

"Millions of guys did that. Are still doing it. Do you think all widows should remain unmarried for the sake of loyalty?"

"I guess not, but when I think of dating, my heart freezes up, and Brian's face comes to mind, like he's watching me. Is his presence telling me something? Maybe he's saying I need to remember him."

"Whew. Those are some heavy thoughts." Van raked his fingers through his hair and slumped against the chair. "I can't tell you what to do, but you need to think about what you would tell Brian if you had died first. Would you expect him to stay single? Consider that, and you'll have the answer for yourself."

Myriad emotions played through her eyes. Wonder. Confusion. Regret. Then a glimmer of hope followed by doubt.

He sighed. What would she decide? Could he be content as her friend if she chose to eschew marriage in honor of her husband's memory?

Chapter Twenty

Silence hung over the table like a wet cloak. Cora sighed and withdrew her hands. Once again, their brainstorming session had become an exploration of her life. Why did Van continuously turn the discussion to her? They had articles to write. Besides, there wasn't enough conversation in the world to unravel her tangled emotions. Guilt and regret were the least of her issues.

She patted Van's arm. "Look. I know you mean well, but I'd rather get back to work." She grinned. "Unless you have a more intriguing topic, let's address school closures and the impact the war has had on the education of the world's children."

He stared at her for a long moment then sent her a curt nod. "We can include the flip side by talking about their being forced to mature earlier than normal because of their exposure to loss, death, privation, and the other ills this war has poured over its inhabitants."

"Growing up before they should. Tragic, isn't it?" Warren, the small child from the orphanage sprang to mind. *Lord, when will this war cease? Please protect Your children.* "The end of the article should include resources for parents and grandparents."

"An excellent idea." He turned his notepad to a fresh sheet and drew two lines down the page creating three columns. With a flourish he labeled the left column School Closures, the middle column Alternatives, and the right column Life's Lessons." Eyebrows raised, he glanced at her. "Sound about right?"

"Sadly, yes." She nibbled on the end of her pencil then scribbled notes under each of the headings. On her own pad, she listed agencies and resources that might help with the research aspect of the story. "You want to divide and conquer or visit these places together?"

"Together. We make a great pair. You think of questions I don't, and vice versa. And your intuition about people is spot on, especially when they're not being forthcoming."

She'd never tire of his encouragement and positive words about her skills. What did that say about her? She wanted to be independent, yet she clung to his compliments as if they were a lifeline. Was she no different than any other woman who needed a man to feel complete?

"If you'll prioritize the list of contacts, I'll set up the appointments." She smirked. "Unless, you want to use your male charm to get a foot in the door."

Van flushed but gave her a sly smile. "Hardly. You're a clever girl and can handle the calls just fine." He jotted more notes on the page then slid the pad toward her.

She added more words then pushed the notebook his way and watched as he scrawled down a few more words. She loved the routine they'd worked out, pushing the page back and forth like a tennis match. Their creativity fed off each other's, ideas flowing faster and faster then building until they merged into a cohesive plan. She was a better writer because of Van. Would she be able to write an article on her own?

Time passed, and the feint and thrust with the sheet of paper slowed until the well of ideas ran dry.

He sat back and tossed his pencil on the table. "Good session." He cocked his head, his expression teasing. "Maybe working with a partner isn't all bad. I've done some of my best stories with you."

Her heart swelled, and she reprimanded herself. Really, Cora. A few kind words, and you becoming a simpering fool. She rubbed her hands on her skirt and winked. Since when did she wink? "Maybe. The jury is still out."

With a chuckle, he closed the book. "I'm beat. How about grabbing some dinner then calling it a night? We can get a jump on the article tomorrow. What are you in the mood to eat?"

"As if we had a choice? I'll have whatever they're serving at the White Stag."

"Will we ever take food for granted again?" He rose and grabbed her jacket from the back of the chair, holding it up so she could slip her arms inside. He stroked her shoulder then gestured for the door. "Shall we?"

"We shall."

They made their way out of the building and ambled down the sidewalk toward the pub. Shoved by the crowd of pedestrians, Cora moved closer to Van. He pulled her hand through the crook of his elbow then wrapped his arm around her shoulder, pressing her to his side. The warmth of his hip seeped through her jacket. Or was she imagining the heat of his body?

She stumbled, and he gripped her tighter. "Are you okay?"

"Yes, sorry. Must pay better attention." She forced a smile. "Or maybe I'm faint with hunger."

His concerned expression turned to one of amusement. "Then it's a good thing we've arrived." He led her into the dim interior of their favorite place to eat.

A young woman with dark hair scraped into a lopsided ponytail jerked her head to the vacant table in the corner. "Seat yerself. I'll be with ya in a moment."

Van lifted his hand in greeting. "Take your time."

Voice mingled with the clink of silverware on stoneware. The greasy aroma of fried fish hung in the air. Cora wrinkled her nose. "Guess we know what's on the menu."

"Maybe we'll get lucky." Hand on her back, he guided Cora through the pub to their table. She shivered at his touch. He pulled a chair out, and she flopped onto the hard seat.

He lowered himself next to her and leaned close, his aftershave enveloping her. "Perhaps we shouldn't have come while the work shifts were changing."

"The change of scenery will do us good, even with all the noise."

"What'll it be, luv?" The waitress stood next to Van, a cheeky smile on her face. "Fish with chips or without?"

"Two orders with. And two cups of tea."

"Nothing from the bar?" The woman put her hands on her hips, eyebrows dancing. "That won't make for much of a night."

"Maybe next time. My lady friend and I are in search of a quiet meal."

Tucking her pencil behind her ear, the woman flicked a glance at Cora. "Suit yerself." With a swish of her skirt, she whirled and strode toward the kitchen.

"Another brokenhearted woman, Van. Can't you see she was pining for you?" Cora giggled, glad to focus on Van and the girl.

"Yeah, I'm sure she's going to cry herself to sleep tonight. I'm pretty sure she's just looking for a good tip." He chuckled. "Enough about her…I used to love to go fishing, and I'd catch my fill of blue gill and bigmouth buffalo. After this is all over, I'm not sure I'll ever look another fish in the eye."

"Bigmouth buffalo is a fish? What a name." She shuddered. "My dad tried to teach us girls how to fish, but Emily's the only one with a penchant for it. Three hours of boredom followed by two minutes of wrestling with a slimy creature. No thanks."

"Fish aren't sli—" He shook his head. "What do you like to do?"

"You'll laugh."

He held up two fingers, then three. "No, I won't. Scout's honor."

"Yeah. Okay, a perfect afternoon for me is being curled up in my mother's wingback chair next to the window, with classical music playing on the Victrola and a Jane Austen book in my hands."

"My grandmother would agree with you." His eyes clouded.

She reached over and squeezed his arm. "You'll see her again."

"I hope so." He cleared his throat. "She and Grandpop aren't getting any younger."

A guffaw punctuated the hum of conversation, then a shrill voice exclaimed, "You're such a scamp."

Cora cringed. She'd know that tone anywhere. Myrtle was here. With hundreds…no…thousands of pubs in London, she'd found her way into the White Stag. How long before she began to work the room and find her and Van?

"Well, Cora Strealer, what a coincidence finding you and Mr. Toppel. I was going to look you up at Broadcasting House."

With a deep breath, Cora pivoted in her chair. Did the woman have radar? "Hello, Myrtle." Overdressed as usual, she wore a bright yellow dress with a wide patent-leather belt cinched at her waist. A tiny yellow hat sat at a jaunty angle on her head. In a plain gray sweater and charcoal skirt, Cora felt like a wren next to a peacock.

Van nodded at Myrtle, his eyes narrow. "Now you don't have to."

"Aren't you going to invite me to join you?"

"No, but thanks for asking."

Her eyes widened, and Cora stifled a laugh. Van seemed unmoved by her charms, and if she was reading the reporter correctly, she wasn't sure how to react.

"Fine. But hear me out. I've notified your editor about your inappropriate relationship, and he seemed none too happy about it. There will be ramifications. You can count on it."

Cora's heart sped up, and she gaped at Myrtle. "How dare you. You've done some despicable things before, but to claim we're acting improperly is low, even for you. You had no right."

Myrtle sneered at her. "It's my duty to ensure my fellow correspondents are adhering to our code of conduct."

"I—"

"Ta ta." With a flip of her wrist, Myrtle waved and threaded her way through the tables and out the door.

"Van, what are we going to do?" Cora's pulse pounded. Everything she'd worked for gone in an instant because of a lie. "I could be fired for this."

"She's out of line. We're not doing anything wrong. Please, don't worry. I will fix this." He ran his finger along her jaw, then sent her a brash smile. "Remember, I'm Superman."

Her chest tight, she forced a smile. "As long as you're not mistaken for Clark Kent."

Chapter Twenty-One

Grasping Cora's hand, Van hurried down the sidewalk toward the Tube station. Their feet crunched on the grit, and he grimaced. How did Londoners stand all the dirt and grime? His job was to go where the stories were, but that didn't mean his heart didn't ache for the clean, fresh outdoors of Iowa. Unfortunately, a man couldn't build a journalistic career in midwestern fields.

The pavement was crowded with factory workers, men in suits, and British and US soldiers. Too bad he didn't have time to sit down with the Americans and reminisce. The bomb waited. Unexploded bomb actually. A UXB as the military referred to them. Only military men and journalists ran *toward* a hazard.

He'd tried to convince Cora that he could cover the situation without her but had been unsuccessful. No surprise, and he didn't blame her. He'd claimed to support her desire to be an investigative reporter and then tried to keep her out of danger. She'd teased him unmercifully about being her Superman.

Hardly. He hadn't been able to contact their editor about Miss O'Malley's report, and now he was leading Cora into possible jeopardy. What kind of guy fails that cataclysmically?

His foot slid in a pile of rubble, and his ankle turned. Pain shot up his calf, and he stopped. Pushed from behind, he hobbled out of the pedestrians' path toward the building, dragging Cora with him. He stood on one leg and massaged the joint.

Concern darkened her face. "What happened? Are you all right?"

"Tweaked my ankle. Give me a minute."

"Should we get you to the hospital?"

"No!"

She drew back, her mouth gaping.

"Sorry." He lowered his voice, and put down his foot, wiggling his ankle. Good. Only a dull throb. "Foolish move. I should have paid better attention. We need to get to that UXB. I have no desire to be scooped."

"Me, neither, but is a story worth risking your health?"

Van quirked his eyebrow. "This from the woman who wouldn't stay home and is heading toward a bomb site."

"Point taken." She flushed and pointed to his ankle. "Are you able to walk?"

"Yes." He took a deep breath and shifted his weight to the injured leg. Clamping his lips, he stifled a groan. He'd suffered worse pain during his college football days, but he'd been younger then. Much younger.

Staying close to the wall of shops, they pushed and bumped their way through the crowd. Several minutes later, they arrived at the stairway that led below ground to the Tube. He gripped the railing and wrapped his free arm around Cora's shoulder. Together, they trudged into the dim recesses to the station.

Moments later, their train rumbled to a stop in front of them. The doors popped open with a hiss, and passengers surged from the cars. The flow slowed, and as travelers on the platform pressed forward to board, Van and Cora swept inside.

He tugged on her hand and jerked his head at a pair of vacant seats. Seeing no women or elderly people who needed to sit, Van dropped onto one of the seats with a sigh. His ankle ached, but the initial sharp pain had dissipated. A reporter with a bum leg was useless. He had to recover. With any luck, the injury was minor, and he'd have full use of his limb after a night's rest.

"How are you feeling?" Cora's voice was low and melodic.

"Better, now that I'm seated. I don't think the damage is serious." He sent her an encouraging smile. "But I'll need my Lois Lane to take lead on the story. I can be your wingman."

"Wingman?" She shook her head. "I'm not familiar with that term."

"That's right, your husband was navy. The word is used by the air force for the guy in the plane behind and on the outside of the lead plane. A pilot who supports another pilot in a potentially dangerous situation."

Her face brightened. "Perfect. And I can return the favor sometime."

"I'll hold you to your promise." He looked forward to redeeming the pledge.

The doors slammed, and the train chugged out of the station, shimmying and bumping along the tracks. He swayed, and his body pressed into Cora's side. They were packed in closer than a family in a Morrison shelter. Which wasn't necessarily a bad thing. Her warmth permeated his sleeve, and her perfume filled his nose. Something floral.

Miles passed, the train stopping at three more stations, gorging and disgorging passengers. Van rubbed his forehead. Would a bus have been faster? How could a reporter scoop another when he was stuck taking public transportation. A mirthless laugh slipped out. Would the public appreciate a story about the woes of a newspaperman?

A grinding noise then a screech. The subway ground to a halt, car lights flickering. Cora grabbed his arm, her eyes wide. "What happened?"

Crackling from overhead, then the lights went out. Someone screamed. Shouts of confusion filled the car.

Cora's grip on his arm tightened to a stranglehold, nearly cutting off circulation to his fingers. He patted her hand. "Stay put and don't panic. There are plenty of others who will take care of that for us."

She giggled, and her fingers loosened.

Good. Now, if he could calm the rest of the passengers.

"Excuse me! Folks!" Van raised his voice above the hubbub. "Could I have your attention, please?"

The din lessened then ceased.

"Thank you. Is anyone hurt?"

Silence.

"No? That's excellent. This is frightening, but I'm sure the gents running the train will have us on our way in no time. We must be patient."

"Who are you?" A timid voice broke the darkness.

"No one of consequence. My name is Van Toppel, and I'm a reporter with the United Press. On my way to a story as a matter of fact. Who else is here?"

"Johnny Miller."

"Sadie Churchill. No relation."

Laughter swept through the subway, and more passengers announced themselves.

Cora nestled close to him, slipping her hand through his arm. "You're wonderful. Thank you for setting us at ease."

His chest swelled. Apparently, he had another chance to protect her. "Let's take our mind off things, shall we? I, for one, am going to think about after the war to a time when I'm outside on a gorgeous, sunny day, wind blowing through the wheat fields."

"A beautiful picture that I'd like to experience someday. Until this war, I took my food for granted." Cora sighed. "No more. I wouldn't mind seeing acres and acres of corn or soybeans or potatoes…well, maybe not potatoes."

"I've had my fill of them, too." He chuckled and stroked her silky hair, an action he wouldn't be brave enough to try in the light. "Perhaps you could visit Iowa, and I could give you a tour of my grandparents' farm."

"I'd like that."

Was that a tremble he detected in her voice? A vision of her wandering the endless fields under a cloudless blue sky crowded his mind. Her blonde hair shimmering in the sunlight as she smiled at him. Sparkling blue eyes dancing in delight.

"Van?"

"Hmm?"

"You were in Iowa, weren't you?" Amusement colored her words.

"Yeah." He wouldn't tell her she was also there. "Did you visit New Hampshire?"

She leaned closer. "Yes. The sun reflecting off the lake with mountains towering in the background. I miss my mountains."

He frowned. She'd hate the flatness of where he lived. Iowa's Hawkeye Point and other peaks were far from his home.

The overhead lights glimmered then doused. Moments later, illumination filled the car. Passengers cheered and applauded. Van hugged Cora to himself as the subway began to chug forward. "Finally. We need to prepare ourselves that the story on the UXB is being covered. I would imagine word of one of those beasts gets out quickly."

"We have our own story to tell."

"That we do."

Minutes passed, and the locomotive picked up speed, rattling and bucking on the tracks. Then squealing brakes, and the train pulled into the next station. Van helped Cora to her feet, and they followed their fellow passengers from the car. Feet thundering on the cement steps, the crowd ascended above ground.

Van squinted in the sunlight and glanced around to get his bearings. The lack of street signs made finding locations tricky, but years of growing up with few landmarks had taught him well. "This way." He turned north, and they hurried along the pavement toward a small park. About thirty people milled around at the entrance while gesturing to a pair of uniformed men peering into a deep hole, presumably at the errant bomb.

"You're a bit late, Mr. Toppel."

Van's head whipped toward the voice.

Smirk on her face, Myrtle O'Malley stood at the edge of the group. "I'm surprised a newspaperman of your caliber wasn't here sooner. Perhaps your partner is slowing you down."

Beside him, Cora tensed, but remained mute.

"Congratulations on scooping us, Miss O'Malley. We'll find something. There are plenty of stories to go around."

Her sneer wavered, then she set her jaw, eyes glittering. "Congratulations are in order for you as well. I wasn't sure if you two were still employed."

Van's stomach fell. Had their editor indicated to the woman that he planned to fire Cora and him? He needed to fix the situation. Pronto.

Chapter Twenty-Two

Two days later, Cora stood by the window in a large room in Broadcasting House. She waved her hand in an effort to clear the heavy, gray cigarette smoke that swirled in front of her face. Dozens of journalists paced and chatted among themselves waiting for the London bureau chief to show up. He'd promised an announcement, and many of the reporters were making wagers as to the topic.

Van waited in the far corner with two men he'd known in Iowa. His laughter carried to her location, and she couldn't help but smile at the sound. He'd been a good sport during their run-in with Myrtle, acting as if he didn't have a care in the world despite her insinuation that he and Cora would be out of a job in the very near future.

Had he contacted their editor as promised? If they were fired, he'd find a job in a flash because of his reputation. She, on the other hand, would be relegated to covering graduation parties in New Hampshire if she managed to get hired at any newspaper. She wasn't exactly Clare Hollingworth or Martha Gellhorn.

Cora's gaze shot to the doorway. More reporters. She glanced at the large clock hanging near the front of the room. Ten fifteen. What was holding up the chief? He'd tan the hide of any reporter who missed a deadline. She sighed and patted her hair as she studied her colleagues.

Cigarettes clamped between their lips, eyes squinting under Brylcreemed hair, the men wore identical gray slacks and light blue or white button-down shirts, ties loosened at the neck. The room was stifling, so few wore sport jackets. Was there an unwritten uniform code among the male reporters?

A half-dozen women also waited, Myrtle among them. Cora watched the woman through her peripheral vision. Clinging to a tall, Gary Cooper-looking man, Myrtle simpered and smiled at the circle of guys surrounding her. She was a good writer. Why did she think she had to act the part of a flirt to get noticed? Surely, the men didn't take her seriously with her Sunday-go-to-meeting outfits and obsequious pandering.

"What's your bet about the announcement?" A stocky man with a two-day growth of whiskers on his jaw, sidled up next to Cora. Bloodshot eyes peered at her from under shaggy, black eyebrows. "Must be big if he's making us cool our heels."

She shrugged at the man. Nick? Norman? Nathan. From the one of the California papers. "Guess we'll know soon enough."

"The boys and me think he's going to tell us about the invasion. Everybody knows it's coming, but where is up for grabs."

Cora's reporter senses prickled. Van had assured her the campaign wouldn't happen for another three or four months. Had he gotten bad intel? "Why would the military tell us about it? The Allies may as well send Hitler a telegram and avoid the middleman of the news agency."

"Part of their strategy to keep him guessing. Propaganda and all that. Reporters have proven useful during the war, so they'll keep using us as long as we fit in their agenda."

"Canny."

He looked her up and down, a smirk etched on his face. "Aren't you that gal who's working with Toppel? How'd he get so lucky?"

"Not luck, Nate." Van towered over the man. "Good business, pure and simple."

"Didn't see you there. When did you sneak in?"

Van rolled his eyes. "Been here the whole time. Same as you. If you were more observant, you might be a better journalist."

Cora stifled a smile and met Van's gaze over Nate's head.

"Hey, that's not a sporting thing to say." Nate frowned and clenched his fists. "I'm a great reporter."

"Whatever you say. Now, why don't you go bother someone else, like Miss O'Malley? I'm sure she could use your sage wisdom."

Nate's face brightened. "An excellent idea." He put two fingers to his forehead in salute and bowed. "Please excuse me, Miss Strealer."

"Certainly, Mr....?"

"Wellington. Like the beef."

"Wellington. Good day." Cora blew out a deep breath. "Thank you for saving me."

"You owe me another one. I'm keeping tally, you know."

"So am I." She sent him an impudent grin then sobered. "Nate says the invasion is going to be soon. What do you think?"

He jerked his head toward the group he'd been talking to. "The guys were speculating about the same possibility. Perhaps the military is more prepared than they've led us to believe. I'm sure they want Hitler and his cronies to believe they can't beat him."

"Eisenhower's promotion in January to commanding general, European Theatre of Operations is going to make a difference. He's a dark horse that no one thought would amount to anything. I believe he has a number of tricks up his sleeve."

"The Allies seem to be making headway in the Pacific, too. The Japanese won't go down easy, but we'll get the best of them."

"A large offensive needs to occur to turn the tide. Show Hitler we mean business. Bombing the German cities is one thing, but the Allies need to take back lost ground." Her lips trembled. "So much loss of life."

"I often wonder what our children and grandchildren will say about us."

"They—"

Commotion at the door signaled the entrance of the bureau chief. Cora watched him stride to the front of the room. Her eyebrows shot up. Martha Gellhorn followed, close on his heels. She leaned toward the man and whispered in his ear. He nodded then gestured for her to remain in position.

Cora would give anything to have ten minutes with the woman who'd married the volatile Ernest Hemingway yet still managed to climb the ranks among the correspondents. Respected among the men as well as the women, Martha had made a name for herself.

The chief held up his hands. "All right, gang. Quiet down, and listen close. I'm only going to say this once."

As if a light switch had been turned off, talking ceased. Not a word was spoken, and every pair of eyes were riveted to the man. Beside her, Van stood ramrod straight, the muscle in his jaw jumping as he clenched his teeth. Why the tension? Was he privy to the information?

"Worst kept secret in Europe is the invasion that Ike's gonna lead. Best kept secret is the location. Calais is the decoy, and it's our job to leak just enough for the Axis to figure that's where the boys are headed. Got it?"

As one, heads bobbed in agreement.

"We've been allotted a handful of reporters to accompany the troops during the real campaign, so Cronkite, Capa, Boyle, Liebling, and Riggs, you're with me. The rest of you, get to work. You've got your orders." He pointed at Van. "And Toppel, I've got something else planned for you."

Disappointment swept the room in one low groan.

Cora shook her head and stamped her foot. "Typical. No women on the list. Of all the misogynistic, shortsighted—"

"Why are you surprised?" Van lifted a shoulder. "Women aren't allowed in combat."

"A ridiculous rule if ever I heard one."

"Toppel, are you coming?" The bureau chief glared at them.

He held up his hand. "Be right there, sir."

"Leave the dame or lose the assignment."

"Yes, sir." He grabbed her in a quick hug and pressed a kiss on her forehead. "I've got to go. I'll be in touch. Stay safe."

"But—"

He pivoted and shoved his way through the milling crowd and disappeared through the door.

Cora clenched her fists and blinked away the angry tears that threatened to spill down her cheeks. If she cried, none of the men would take her seriously. She turned and stared through the glass pane at the pedestrians below. Intent on their business, they looked neither left nor right, pushing themselves forward, like ants at a picnic.

Should she pack her bags and take the next flight home? Did the stories she'd written with Van matter? Or were they fluff pieces that no one read in lieu of the casualty reports or articles about the victories and defeats suffered by both sides. Would she ever get to cover real news?

She huffed a breath and whirled, bumping into Miss Gellhorn. "Oh! My apologies. I didn't see you." Her face heated. The woman must think her a bumbling idiot. So much for making an impression on her heroine.

"Quite all right. I noticed you speaking with Van Toppel. Do you know him well?"

"Uh…yes…he and I were teamed on a series of articles."

"And now you've been relegated with staying behind. What a pip, eh?" Martha's lip curled. "We gals are just as capable as the guys, yet we're constantly overlooked in their favor." She sneered. "I'm penning a letter to the authorities telling them what I think about their silly rules. We're correspondents, same as the boys. We shouldn't have to beg for the right to serve as the eyes for those in America who can't see what's happening for themselves."

"Exactly. An infuriating position for us to be in. I hope your letter makes a difference."

"Between you and me, I don't plan to wait for permission. I'll get there by hook or by crook, and no one can stop me."

Cora's eyes widened. "You'll lose your accreditation."

"But I'll have my story." Martha grinned and crossed her arms. "I usually manage to gain forgiveness for my, shall we say, indiscretions with regard to the mandates. Guess I'll have to polish up on my apology." She winked. "You might consider taking a few risks. Feel free to use my name if you get into a bind. Or better yet, use your connection to that handsome Mr. Toppel."

"Thank you, but I haven't decided what I'm going to do."

"Suit yourself. Well, I'm off. Got some reconnaissance to do." She flipped her wavy, brown hair over her shoulder then marched past the men and out the door.

Was Martha really planning to go into combat? To infiltrate the troops and cover the invasion? Cora's heart banged inside her chest. After talking to the intrepid Miss Gellhorn, she no longer wished to crawl home, tail between her legs. But did she have what it took to risk her career and her life for a story?

Van. He'd put the kibosh on any plan she set in motion to break the rules. She couldn't tell him. He had too much honor not to try to stop her or inform the higher-ups if he couldn't convince her to remain in London. If she tried to follow the invasion, what would her stunt do to their friendship?

How were the rest of the reporters dealing with their rejection? A stop by the typing room might prove informative. She smiled and rushed from the room. Trotting down the hall, she could hear the cacophony of heated voices before arriving at her destination. She entered and saw Martha sitting in the corner, seemingly engrossed in her notes. In reality, the woman was probably absorbing every conversation.

"Listen, I'm headed out soon for an assignment the chief gave me, but I'll keep you posted. Meanwhile, I should have called you two days ago."

Cora whirled. Van was still here and on the phone with someone. His editor?

"Right. Hey, did you get a call from Myrtle O'Malley? Journalist from *Collier's*. Yeah, that's her. Did she tell you Miss Strealer and I are being…uh…inappropriate? Well, her story is hogwash. Cora is an excellent reporter. You can see that from her work. Anyway, we're not doing anything wrong…I do care for her, more than I probably should, but we're on the up and up. You gotta believe me."

Her jaw dropped, and she covered her mouth. Did he just claim he had feelings for her? Why did he see the need to continue the act? Surely, any admission of romance could jeopardize their careers. Or was he counting on his posh new assignment to smooth over any bumps?

Chapter Twenty-Three

Hunched over the desk, Van pressed the telephone receiver closer to his ear. He should have found another place from which to make the call. The bedlam behind him nearly drowned out his editor's voice on the other end of the phone. He was disappointed at not being tapped for the invasion force, but grousing didn't change the situation. Didn't the other guys understand there was enough news to go around?

A dry laugh escaped. He used to be like the others, pushing down colleagues to be first in line for the best assignments. Mere months ago, he'd have complained if he wasn't picked for the invasion team. What had changed?

Cora's face appeared in his mind, and he smiled. Not what, but who. His sweet, beautiful partner was the difference in his life. Not that he was lackadaisical, but a level of contentment now permeated his existence, and never in a million years would he have anticipated his transformation. If they knew, the other reporters would think he'd gone soft. They ribbed him enough about his co-authoring situation.

Too bad whatever assignment the bureau chief was giving him didn't include Cora. He'd popped into the chief's office after the man had barked at him to hurry, then he'd waved Van off with a "Come back later" and a sneer. Not typically friendly, the man was now in a chronic bad mood.

"When are you going to know where you're going?" Mr. Atkinson's tinny voice crackled through the phone lines. "I need to figure out how to cover your column."

He shrugged and then rolled his eyes. His editor couldn't see his actions. "Dunno. Later is all he said. Once he finishes with the guys he's sending with the troops, he'll probably collar me. I can call you afterwards." Van raked his fingers through his hair. "Cora can handle our column. No need to pair her with anyone else."

"Is that jealousy in your voice, Toppel?" A warm chuckle came through the line. "I know she's capable. I hired her. Remember? You were the skeptic, but that has all changed if you're to be believed."

"Why wouldn't you believe me?" Van frowned and squirmed in the chair. "I've spilled my guts over a phone line in a room filled with reporters."

"No need to get testy. I'm yanking your chain. What you do in your personal life is none of my business as long as you're not letting your *relationship* get in the way of doing your job. I'm well aware of Miss O'Malley's reputation as a pot-stirrer, so I put little stock in what she has to say."

Van blew out a deep breath. "That's a relief. I'm persuasive, but pleading my case over the telephone has limitations."

Atkinson guffawed. "You mean you can't use those puppy-dog eyes of yours like you can with the ladies."

"Very funny."

"That's me. A real comedian. Anyway, I wish the chief had asked me about reassigning you. Your shared stories with Miss Strealer have been a big hit with our readership. We're receiving hundreds of letters about the articles, some of which wonder whether you two are seeing each other, so I guess your little tête-à-tête might work out to our favor. I'd be a fool not to let you date."

"Who dates in the middle of a war? Worrying about when the next bomb is going fall puts a damper on a night out. We spend lots of time together, but it's for research, interviews, and brainstorming."

"Yeah, that would be a problem, but you're a smart boy, Van. You'll figure something out. The more I think about it, you should add this angle to your stories. Give the readers a peek into your life with Miss Strealer."

"Boss, have you forgotten I've been pulled off our series?"

Atkinson growled. "How long before you ship out? Surely, you can pencil-whip a couple of pieces and get them to me by tomorrow."

"You want me to pull an all-nighter?"

"There's a war on. Who sleeps?"

"I try to get the luxury of a couple of hours." Van let sarcasm paint his words. "But I won't look like much when this is all over."

"Then it's a good thing your appearance doesn't matter to me." Atkinson's voice warmed. "In all seriousness, you do need to get some rest. You're no good to me if you kill yourself through exhaustion, but could you squeeze one piece out tonight? Four hundred words."

"I can swing that unless the chief puts me on a boat or plane tonight." Van's heart lifted. Another piece for their column meant time with Cora before he left. Would he be able to focus on the article rather than his lovely colleague? "Any chance of getting me assigned to the group covering the invasion?"

"No way. That decision sits directly with the chief, and it seems he's already made his choice. Good luck with the other assignment."

"Yeah. Thanks, anyway." Van hung up the phone with a clatter. The noise in the room had dissipated. He glanced around and smiled. Most of the boys had cleared out, probably in search of the next great scoop. No sign of Cora. Had she left the building, too? Might be tough to find her.

Van jumped up and trotted out of the room and through the hall peeking in each room. Nothing. He clattered down the stairs. The White Stag first then her boardinghouse. Where else would she go?

He pushed open the door, and a breeze stroked his face, cooling his hot skin. Blotting the perspiration at his hairline and on his upper lip, with his sleeve, he glanced left then right. Which direction? A flash of yellow across the street caught his attention, and he cringed. Miss O'Malley?

Nope. Cora talked with three women and their children. One of the little girls wore a dandelion-yellow blouse. His chest eased. *Thank You,*

Lord, for helping me find her. He parked himself on the bench at the curb and watched Cora interact with the ladies.

Her smile was gracious and genuine, and the women seemed intent upon her words. They nodded and periodically responded. What story was she chasing? One for their column or had she already struck out on her own? Would she even miss him when he was gone?

Chapter Twenty-Four

Cora waved as the trio of women and their children headed out of the park. Their presence had been a godsend. Mind racing with confusion after having Van selected for a special assignment, hearing him claim he cared about her more than he should to their editor, and then her conversation with Miss Gellhorn, she'd burst out of Broadcasting House uncertain where to turn.

The youngster's giggles and joyous expressions had drawn her across the street to watch them play. In many ways, she longed for the simple life of childhood. Her parents had taken care of her every need, and her sisters had been her best friends. Until high school when teenage angst overrode familial bonds, and they'd grown apart.

Her lips trembled. Would she live to see Emily and Doris? Would they survive this war and come home?

Greeted warmly by the kids' mothers, she spoke to them about everything and nothing. Glad to have the day off from the factory free of responsibilities, the women regaled her with their experiences at home and at the plant. Working ten to twelve hours, their typical day included rising before dawn to do laundry, weed their Victory gardens, go to the market, and myriad other tasks to keep the household running without their husbands.

Despite worry that lurked behind their eyes, they'd joked with each other and her. Did the nations realize the level of sacrifice being made on the home fronts? Especially in countries where being killed in an air raid was a daily concern.

She shook her head and blew out a sigh. Focus on the positive, Cora. You still have a job, a place to live, and more importantly, your life.

A breeze lifted the swings, sending them swaying as if unseen children balanced on the seat and pumped their legs. Cora glanced around. The park had emptied, and she was alone. She grinned. Childhood, here I come.

With a hop, she seated herself on the wooden board and wrapped her fingers around the ropes, their textured surface rough on her palms. Using her toe, she gave herself a push, leaned back to create momentum, then pumped her legs. The wind stroked her cheeks, and tugged at her ponytail with warm fingers. She closed her eyes and unclipped the barrette binding her hair. Flowing freely, her tresses danced around her face tickling her skin.

Higher. Higher. To freedom.

Thank You, God, for simple pleasures.

Her muscles loosened, and her breathing slowed. Birds sang in the trees. "The Lord is my shepherd; I shall not want. He maketh me to lie down in green pastures: He leadeth me beside the still waters. He restoreth my soul." She smiled. The park was green with no water nearby, but King David vocalized what she couldn't in his Psalm.

"Yea, though I walk through the valley of the shadow of death, I will fear no evil." Why couldn't she remember to cling to God's promise? She allowed herself to get caught up in strife and worry, letting fright of the future to strip her of peace. He was in control, yet she tried to push her will into the forefront.

"Forgive me, Father. I messed up again. Help me follow Your plan and not mine."

"Cora!"

Her eyes popped open. Van trotted toward her. Was he part of God's plan?

She stopped her legs, slowing her movement, until she was able to catch her foot on the ground.

"Don't quit on my account. I could join you."

"Nah, that's okay. I've wasted enough time, but it felt good to put the day on hold." She cocked her head. "I thought you'd be in with the bureau chief. What's up?"

"Yeah, he's too busy talking to the guys who are headed out with the troops. Said he'd see me later." He shuffled his feet, looking like a small child who'd been caught red handed in the cookie jar. "Anyway, I should have taken care of Miss O'Malley's insinuations two days ago, and I'm sorry for being lax about it, but I called Mr. Atkinson. No need to worry about our jobs. In fact, he wants you to continue with our column while I'm on special assignment."

"That's wonderful, Van. Thanks for handling that." Her heart thumped at the gleam in his eye. He did seem to care, but were his feelings as strong as he alluded to during his phone call? "I guess I was silly to worry." Once again, he'd proven to be a hero, taking care of her needs and seeming thrilled to do so.

"Happy to do it." He laced his fingers with hers and pulled her off the swing. "I should get back in case the chief is ready to talk, but will you wait for me? We could grab something to eat. Might be our last chance for a while."

Her stomach clenched, and she pinned a smile on her face. More time with Van would only make their separation harder because she loved him. She'd been fighting the realization for days, but she may as well admit her feelings. At least to herself. She certainly couldn't tell him. Mutual careers in journalism were not enough in common to make a relationship. Besides, she'd already decided a second marriage wasn't in the cards.

"No, but thanks for the offer. I'm bushed, so I'm going to head home and try to pick up something on the way." She squeezed his hand then released his fingers. "I'd say good luck, but you won't need it. Godspeed, and we'll catch up when you get back, unless, of course, you do such a fabulous job they promote you." She clamped her lips over her ramblings then pressed a quick kiss to his cheek, inhaling the scent she'd grown to know. Before she wilted in his arms, she whirled and hurried away.

"Cora!"

Without turning, she waved her hand in farewell. If she saw his face, she'd lose her nerve, and that would never do. She strained her ears for the sound of his pounding feet chasing her.

Nothing.

Cora straightened her spine and clutched her pocketbook. She was on her own now. The path she took was up to her. She'd continue to fulfill her obligations and submit their column, but she needed to do more, write stories to make the people at home sit up and take notice about what the young men and women were doing to keep them safe.

Martha was right. Time for Cora to grab her career by the horns. She'd find out where the ships were transporting the troops for the invasion and get herself onboard.

A pair of Red Cross girls bumped into her and kept walking.

"Excuse me." She frowned as she watched them turn the corner. Did they not see her? Or were they so intent on their destination, she was invisible.

"That's what I'll do!" She snapped her fingers and grinned. Doctors and nurses in the medical corps as well as the Red Cross would accompany the troop transport. She'd tag along. Her first-aid training might be rusty, but she maintained the knowledge and would be an asset to the campaign.

Now, to find a uniform.

<hr>

Tugging at the snug blue jacket of the Red Cross uniform, Cora slung her satchel over her shoulder as she rushed toward the dock from the bus stop. She gripped the billed cap that also didn't quite fit, the blouse restricting her arm from lifting completely. Compliments of a friend of a friend at the boardinghouse, the outfit had seen better days. She'd had to pin the skirt to keep it closed and prayed the fastener wouldn't burst. Why couldn't the uniform consist of a comfortable pair of denim slacks, a more practical solution for carrying stretchers and crawling over terrain to care for the injured?

She rolled her eyes. In every role held by women during the war, they were expected to look feminine and chic. A ridiculous notion.

After securing the outfit, she'd returned to Broadcasting House against her better judgment, but her fear of running into Van had been baseless. He was nowhere to be found on the premises. Like Miss Gellhorn had done earlier, Cora sequestered herself in the corner of the busy newsroom and pretended to review her notes. Ignored, she sat and absorbed every kernel of information the boys bandied about. Thirty minutes after arriving, she had the location of the ships that would soon make their way across the Channel toward France.

Racing home, she'd thrown a few clothes, her toothbrush, and a comb into a bag then ran to catch the bus that would take her to the Waterloo station. Breath ragged and heart pounding, she'd arrived mere minutes before the train pulled out. The two-hour ride gave her time to recover, but her pulse still hammered.

Eisenhower's plan was bold, a campaign that would encompass thousands of ships and millions of young men. D-Day, as her colleagues referred to the day the attack would commence, was dependent on the weather and the effect it would have on the spring tides. Poor conditions meant the supreme commander would scrap the plans until the next full moon. Could the Allies risk waiting another thirty days? What would Hitler do in the meantime?

She approached the Southampton docks and surveyed the chaos. Hundreds of ships lay at anchor, stretching to the distant horizon. Vehicles trundled back and forth delivering supplies to waiting soldiers and sailors who loaded the items in the hold. The briny air chilled Cora's face. Metal clanked and banged, and men shouted. Engines roared, and sea gulls laughed at the commotion.

"Watch out, miss!"

Cora sidestepped a pair of American GIs, privates if she remembered how many stripes indicated which rank, wrestling with a stack of boxes. "Sorry!" She stopped. "Can you tell me where the Red Cross folks check in?"

The taller of the two men sneered. "Ain't you got your orders?"

Her face warmed. "Uh, yes, in my bag somewhere, but uh…"

"Look for the ships with the red cross painted on the side. Pick one. That'll get you started."

"Thank you. And uh…again, sorry."

He shrugged and gestured for his partner to grab one end of a large crate. Backs to her, they walked toward the nearest ship, a behemoth that rose high above her head, perhaps as much as a three- or four-story building. Nothing like the pleasure crafts used on the lake at home, the ship featured towers, masts, and massive guns.

She shuddered. What had she gotten herself into?

Chapter Twenty-Five

With a tight grip on her pocketbook and satchel, Cora squinted into the sun and studied the dock. Like ants at a picnic, men in uniform crawled over the ships, ducking in and out of openings, up and down the ropes, and on and off the gangplanks. Intent on their work, no one looked her way. She needn't worry about getting caught as an unauthorized person because none of the men seemed to care who else was on the premises.

She straightened her spine. Her gaze swept the undulating crowd of men. Was she the only woman here? Where were the hospital ships?

Buck up, girl. Miss Gellhorn would have already bluffed her way onto the ship. Cora nodded to herself and took a deep breath. She marched to the nearest gangplank, waited until it cleared, and placed her foot onto the metal passageway. The bridge dipped then rose, and she stumbled. Grabbing at the rail, she steadied herself.

From the dock the ship appeared unmoving, yet the steel giant bobbed in the water like the small boats at home. How was that possible?

"Keep moving, lady. We got work to do," a deep voice interrupted her thoughts from behind.

"Of course." Cora glanced over her shoulder. Several scowling GIs held crates. "Oh, I'm sorry." Face heating, she scampered to the end of the gangplank then stepped onto the ship and pressed herself against the wall. The men nodded to her as they carried their loads on board.

Her gaze darted back and forth. Which way to go? Tears pricked the backs of her eyes, and her pulse raced. Perspiration broke out along her hairline. Had she come this far only to chicken out? No. Miss Gellhorn might never know of her exploits, but she wanted to make the woman proud. To do this crazy stunt on behalf of all the female correspondents who were stuck in dead-end assignments. She would do this.

Lips pressed together, she lifted her chin and strode along the deck, threading her way through stacks of matériel and servicemen. She spied a tall soldier carrying a sheaf of papers and barking at a group of men huddled in the corner. With a glance at the patch on his arm, she set her jaw and made her way to him. She stood behind him, cringing at the colorful language that spewed from his mouth.

He turned and barreled into her, nearly knocking her off her feet. His pages fell as he grabbed her arms and kept her from falling. A snarl curled his lips, and his face darkened. "Red Cross dames below deck! You gals have got to stay out of the way while we load these babies."

She shrank under his thunderous glare. "I'm…uh…new. I just arrived and wasn't sure where to report."

His left eyebrow shot up as he released her. "Your order should contain that information. If you can't follow directions, you shouldn't be here." He bent and retrieved his scattered papers, then rose, towering over her again. He jerked his head toward the rear of the ship. "There's an entrance on the port side of the stern. Head inside, then take the first set of ladders, then follow the corridor until—"

"Port side? Stern?" Her breath hitched. The man was speaking a foreign language. At this rate, she'd be lucky to find anything.

He rolled his eyes and blew out a loud breath. "Right. You're a civilian. Port side is the left side if you're facing the bow…er…front of the ship. Starboard is on the right. The stern is the back. Stairs are called ladders; floors are called decks; and the walls bulkheads. Clear?"

"Um, sure." She forced a smile so he wouldn't see how intimidated she appeared. Would all the men be as uncivil? "As you were saying?"

"I'll give it to you in terms you understand. Go to the back of the boat on the side closest to the dock. Go through the hatch…uh…doorway and take the first set of stairs to the next deck below. Walk along the hallway until you see a large room with lots of tables and chairs. That's the dining area, and the Red Cross has set up there to check in their folks."

"Thank you." She spoke to his back as he pivoted and stalked away. "Well, not the warmest of welcomes, but at least I know where I'm going." She turned and followed his directions, pushing her way through the mayhem. Her head thrummed with the shouts and constant banging of metal against metal. Would that noise accompany them during the entire journey?

She rubbed her forehead. Now that she knew where the Red Cross authorities were, she could determine the best place to stay out from under their watchful eyes. Despite disguising herself as one of their members, she'd stopped short of securing falsified orders. She'd managed to bluff her way onto the ship without them, and with any luck no one would ask to see them once the transport was underway. *Keep us safe, Father.*

Why should He listen to her prayers? She was asking Him to bless her sinful deeds, and that He'd never do. She didn't deserve His mercy or protection. *Forgive me, Lord.*

Silence.

Her lips trembled. She was putting herself in harm's way for a story after lecturing Van on the foolishness of such a deed. She was a hypocrite. Would she live to submit her article or sink to the bottom of the sea, leaving her friends and family to wonder about her fate? Did Emily suffer such fears during her missions? None of the family knew what she was doing, only that her work was hush-hush, as the British liked to say. But with her knowledge of the French language and culture, Cora had no doubt she was in France or had been at some point. *Please keep her safe, Lord.*

Hand braced against the ship, Cora picked her way across the swaying deck. A shrill whistle cut through the mayhem below, and her head spun toward the noise. Why had she looked? It wasn't as if the sound was for her. More likely, some crewman trying to grab the attention of one of his shipmates. Her guilt was making her jumpy.

A burst of fuchsia darted through the crowd. No. It couldn't be. Cora's heart pounded. She gripped the railing. But who else would wear such bright colors? She squinted in the setting sun and shielded her eyes, following the path of whomever was dressed in the flashy outfit. The sea of green uniforms parted, and she caught a glimpse of a pink pillbox hat set on shining mahogany hair. Her chest tightened.

The woman looked up, and Cora froze. Myrtle O'Malley. In the flesh. Was she trying to sneak on board? Or had she managed to get permission? No. Women weren't allowed in combat. And in a dress like that, stealth was out of the question. What on earth was she doing here?

Myrtle sashayed through the chaos, simpering and speaking to the men, many of whom ogled her as she passed. She reached a jeep, and one of the soldiers jumped out of the vehicle, a huge smile on his face. He grabbed Myrtle into a bear hug and lifted her from the ground as she wrapped her arms around his neck. They embraced for a long moment, then he set her down and kissed her cheek. Who was that man? He'd embraced her, but his kiss seemed anything but ardent. A relative? A friend? A source?

Had Myrtle managed to scoop her and Van without stepping onto a ship? The soldier gestured toward the ship Cora was on, and she ducked out of sight. If Myrtle saw her, she'd report Cora to the authorities without a second thought. Best to get below deck before her cover was blown.

Breathless at nearly being caught, she continued through the hold, studying the tiny signs affixed to the wall…uh…bulkhead beside each door. One marked Supplies. She looked left and right, and seeing no one, yanked open the door and slipped inside.

The closet was perhaps four feet square with floor-to-ceiling shelves crammed with bottles, cloths, brushes, and buckets. A collection of mops and brooms leaned against the wall in one corner. She closed the door, and the tiny room was cloaked in darkness. Did she really want to spend the next twelve hours or more shoehorned in this black hole? How long before she ran out of air? Perhaps, she'd only stay until they cast anchor. Should she try to blend in with the other Red Cross girls or secrete herself in a succession of hiding places?

Amanda would tell her to hide in the open. Her friend would say as long as she looked confident, her ruse would be believed. They'd successfully cut class in high school with bravado. Why not use the same technique?

Cora set down her bags, opened the door to let in a crack of light so she could see, then grabbed a bucket and overturned it on the floor. She shut the door and groped in the darkness until she found the pail, seating herself on the hard steel. Muffled voices and footsteps passed in the corridor. Her shoulders tensed. Would the door be unceremoniously jerked open? How would she explain her presence? What would Van do?

His face sprang to mind, and she grinned. He'd bluff his way through the situation with charm and aplomb. He might be a farmer at heart, but he was a natural-born salesman.

Her smile wavered. He was going to be angry when he learned what she'd done. First, he'd be upset because she'd scooped him. Then he'd be dismayed that she'd put herself in danger. Would he have even the smallest bit of pride for her daring do?

Probably not.

Didn't matter. He watched out for his career, and she could handle her own. She had no doubt Miss Gellhorn was on one of the ships. She'd insinuated as much during their last conversation. If Martha could do this, so could she. The journey would be interminable if she argued with herself across the entire Channel.

Time crawled, and Cora pinched herself to remain awake. The gentle rocking of the ship combined with the warmth and darkness of the closet made her drowsy. Had she nodded off?

Rumbling started beneath her feet, and the floor vibrated. Noise outside the door ceased. The ship was getting underway. Her heart jumped into her throat. She was heading into war…into battle. Her stomach roiled, and her lunch threatened to reappear.

There was no turning back.

Chapter Twenty-Six

Another glance at the clock, and Van pursed his lips. Only two minutes later than the last time he checked the time. He shoved his hands into his pockets and marched to the doorway. The corridor was empty. Returning to the room, he coughed and waved away the cigarette smoke that permeated the room. Movement near the window caught his attention. Two of the correspondents from United Press laughed and pointed at something outside.

Curious.

He nudged his way through the rows of tables holding typewriters until he was behind the men. "Something amusing, guys?"

Mustached with a shaggy head of hair, Edwin Hodgdon chuckled and gestured to the sidewalk across the street where a young boy and his dog performed tricks. "One smart pup. Nice to see something cute for a change."

A correspondent with one of the Idaho papers, Warren Thompson nodded. "I've had my fill of death and destruction. Seemed like a great opportunity to be here, but I'm looking forward to reporting on 4H fairs and town elections."

Hodgdon tugged at his tie. "Yeah, I wouldn't mind a fluff piece or two."

"Or three." Van sighed. "Think I'll run down and give the kid a couple of quid."

Thompson dug into his pocket. "Count me in."

"Me, too." Hodgdon handed him a fistful of coins.

"Righto." Van glanced out the glass and froze. A petite woman in a charcoal-colored suit hurried along the pavement. Blonde hair flowing from under a narrow-brimmed fedora, she ducked her head. An unwieldy satchel hung from her shoulder. Cora?

The woman stopped and watched the performer and his dog, then clapped her gloved hands. She pulled something out of her pocketbook and tucked it into the boy's hand. With a wave, she continued along the sidewalk.

Look up. Look up. Van strained to catch a glimpse of the woman's face.

As if she heard his silent plea, the blonde turned her face skyward.

Not Cora.

Van frowned.

"Everything all right, Toppel?" Hodgdon cocked his head. "You seem enamored with that dish in the gray suit."

"Fine. Yeah, fine." Van tore his eyes from the view and turned. "I'm going to make our contribution to the boy and get going. Good luck on your stories."

"Let us know if you need anything."

"Sure." Van sent them a distracted wave then made his way out of the room and down the stairs. He trotted through the lobby and out the front door. After waiting for traffic to clear, he crossed the street, then pressed the money into the boy's palm. A quick pat of the dog, and he headed down the street in the direction of Cora's lodging.

"Thanks, mister!" The youngster's high-pitched voice sounded awestruck.

Van pressed his lips together. The kid deserved a real childhood, not one in which he had to collect coins on the street. Maybe he'd misread the situation, but the boy's threadbare clothes and haggard appearance seemed to indicate the family was poor and needy. How many other families were out there struggling to provide for themselves?

How had his mood gone from amused to morose in a split second? He shook his head to clear the melancholy thoughts and dodged pedestrians. The streets were more crowded than usual. Was there a story in the making?

He snickered. Always a newsman.

Twenty minutes later, he arrived at Cora's boardinghouse. Five years into the war, yet the brick façade was barely nicked. Sparkling windows crisscrossed with tape featured window boxes filled with pink blooms that bobbed in the breeze. The landlady apparently took pride in keeping the Georgian home pristine and in order.

He climbed the stairs and stepped onto the small columned portico. A pot of flowers sat in the corner by the door. Hand fisted, he knocked on the brightly colored blue door. Tapping his foot, he blew out a breath. What would Cora think about him chasing her down at home? They'd stayed out of each other's personal lives, preferring to meet at Broadcasting House.

Raising his hand to pound again, he paused as footsteps sounded inside. The door swung open. A slender brunette woman, perhaps in her twenties, smiled at him through the screen door. "Yes?"

"I'm…uh…Van Toppel to see Cora Strealer. We…uh…work together. Is she here?"

"No. She's gone. Was she expecting you?"

"Not here…at work. She didn't show up. I'm shipping out, but we're collaborating on one final article, and I need her input."

The woman cocked her head. "Perhaps she'll bring it by on her way out of town."

"What?" Van's eyes widened, and his pulse skipped. "Where is she going?"

"She didn't say, but then she seemed in a big hurry and wasn't in a talkative mood. Maybe she had a bus to catch. All I know is that she packed all her things and told the landlady she could let the room."

"Why didn't she tell me?" He winced at the whining tone in his voice. "I mean…we've been partners, so I thought she'd inform me if she received a new assignment."

"Check with the Red Cross." She started to close the door. "They should be able to help you."

"The Red Cross? Why would they know anything about a reporter?"

"Because she was wearing one of their uniforms, borrowed from one of the girls who lives here."

"But—"

"Look, mister. I've told you all I know. Now, I just got off the night shift and would like to grab some shut-eye."

His face heated. "Of course…I'm sorry…thank you for your help."

The woman yawned and shut the door with a quiet thud.

Mind racing, Van stared at the door for a long moment then pivoted and galloped down the steps. What was Cora doing? Had something happened to make her quit the newspaper business and join the Red Cross? She'd never expressed interest in medicine, but maybe she had a hidden desire that rose to the surface. Overnight? Hardly. There was something else going on.

Where was the Red Cross's London office? He needed to get to the bottom of her disappearance.

Rummaging in his pocket, he retrieved a coin and hurried toward the burgundy-and-glass telephone booth. He shoved the money into the slot and dialed the operator. After a short conversation, he secured the location of the office and disconnected the call. Perspiration trickled down his spine. He wouldn't look like much when he found Cora.

Feet slapping the pavement, he jogged past shops that lined the street. Loud in his ears, his breath came in gasps, and his thighs burned as his legs ate up the distance to the headquarters. He sidestepped the few pedestrians remaining in his path, glad for the agility he'd learned during track-and-field training in high school. Hurdling was probably out of the question, but at least he was beginning to get his rhythm back. With any luck, he wouldn't collapse when he arrived at his destination.

He glanced at his watch. Time was slipping away. He lengthened his stride. Would he find her before he needed to give up the search and work on his assignment? Oh, Cora, where are you?

Five blocks. Four blocks. Almost there. Three blocks. His heart hammered in his chest. Two blocks. Slowing his pace, he took deep breaths and wiped the sweat from his face. Turning the corner, he dropped to a walk as he read the signs on the buildings.

Red Cross: London Headquarters.

Finally. He brushed the wrinkles from his slacks and smoothed his shirt. He raked his fingers through his hair and peered at his reflection in the window. Other than a flushed face, he didn't look too bad. With a deep breath, he pulled open the door and entered the foyer.

Bright and airy, the room was decidedly cooler than outside. A middle-aged woman in a gray-blue seersucker uniform sat behind a massive desk. Stacks of folders covered most of the desk's surface except for the woman's typewriter. She looked up and smiled, her vibrant hazel eyes crinkling at the edges.

"Hello, sir. How may I help you?"

"I telephoned a short time ago, and someone indicated they might be able to help me find my friend."

"Ah, yes. That was me. We don't release information over the phone, and I'm not sure how much I can tell you, but let's give it a go, shall we?"

His breath expelled in a loud gasp. "Sorry, but I'm worried about her, you see, and I'm up against a deadline. I've run all the way here."

She gestured to a beat-up folding chair. "Then you should have a seat and rest." She lifted the phone receiver. "Jenny, can you bring me a cup of tea? Thank you." The woman hung up then folded her hands. "Now, tell me about your friend."

"Her name is Cora Strealer, and she has long, blonde hair, almost the color of ripe wheat, and her eyes are blue." He stood and held his hand below his chin. "She's small, fitting under my chin, like so." Van dropped back into the chair.

"That could be any number of our girls. Does she have any distinguishing marks, a birthmark perhaps?"

"No, but she's quite beautiful."

The woman chuckled. "Also could be any number of our members."

His face warmed as if seared. She must think him an idiot. "Of course. Well, she would have come through here today. One of her housemates saw her this morning in one of your uniforms."

"Hmmm. We've only had two gals join us today, and both were brunettes. Perhaps she joined yesterday? Was Miss Strealer's friend sure it was one of our uniforms?"

"Cora was with me at work all day yesterday, and I didn't quiz the girl heavily. The young woman seemed sure of herself that Cora was in a Red Cross outfit. In fact, she indicated she'd borrowed it from one of the other girls in the house."

"We would have issued her clothing." She shook her head. "Nonetheless, let me check." She slid open the bottom drawer and flipped through the folders one by one, her lips moving as she read the names. Saunders, Shores, Skinner, Smith, Sturdivant, Summers. I'm sorry, sir, but I don't have a file on Miss Strealer."

"I don't understand." Van clenched his hands. "Why would she be wearing a Red Cross uniform if she's not a member of your organization?" A chill swept over him. "Wait. You have hospital ships that are heading out with invasion forces. Where are they?"

"I can't tell you that, sir. It's classified. I've already said too much."

He banged his fists on the desk. "Where!"

She squealed. "Sir, I can have you removed from here."

"I'm sorry, but I'm concerned she's done something foolish. I have to save her."

"I—"

Van held up his hand. "Don't say anything." Which deep water port would they send thousands of ships from?" He snapped his fingers. "Southampton."

The woman's eyes shuttered, but she sent him an imperceptible nod.

His heart soared then fell. He had a location, but the amount of time required to get there would preclude him from submitting an article. He raced from the building. Cora's life took precedence over the newspaper. He'd apologize to his editor later. For now, he had a train to catch.

Chapter Twenty-Seven

Van trudged into Broadcasting House, his satchel over one shoulder. Had God or the British government intervened in his plans to go to Southampton? He'd arrived at Waterloo station, but there was some sort of problem with the tracks, or so the officials said, and the next train wouldn't head south for another three hours. As a result of the delay, common sense intervened, and he'd gone home to pack a bag with clothes, extra notepads, and pencils. He'd decided not to lug the typewriter. No matter how portable the machine was touted to be, it was too bulky and heavy to drag with him.

He'd telegrammed his editor that the expected article would not be forthcoming, and he'd be in touch. Hopefully, the man would understand after all was said and done. Now it was time to speak with the bureau chief, a meeting he dreaded.

The elevator door opened, and he stepped inside. Vacant except for the operator, who smiled. "Good afternoon, Mr. Toppel."

"Afternoon, Barney."

"Any news I should know about?" The elderly man winked and jabbed him with his elbow. "I promise not to tell anyone."

"Not yet, but keep your ear to the ground. Things are heating up." Van sighed. They had the same conversation every day, but he didn't blame the man. A career military man and nearly eighty, Barney had seen his share of action in the Third Burma War, the Six-Day War and the Second Boer War. He probably missed the excitement of being involved.

"Very good, sir." Barney saluted.

They arrived at Van's floor, and Barney gestured for him to exit the elevator. "Good day to you. I hope you're able to scoop the other boys."

"Me, too." Van smiled and strode down the corridor. Did the man say that to all the journalists?

The hubbub in the correspondents' room seemed louder than usual. He picked up his pace and walked through the doorway. Shoulder to shoulder at the typewriters, men and women hammered out stories while others waited their turn and hunkered over notepads and scraps of paper. The war was coming to a head, and everyone knew it.

"Toppel!"

His head whipped around.

Chomping on a cigar, looking very much like England's prime minister, the bureau chief beckoned him from near the window.

The moment of truth had arrived. Sweat broke out along Van's hairline and dampened his shirt. "Yes, sir." He pushed his way through the crowd, his nose wrinkling at the fetid smell of cigarette smoke, perspiration, and old food.

"There's been a change. Riggs was injured in a train accident. Derailment at one of the stations. Broke his leg, so he's down for the count. You'll take his place."

Van's eyes widened, and his breath hitched. "Uh…thank you, sir. I appreciate the opportunity." He shook his head. What if he'd gone to Southampton?

"Let's go to my office, and I'll give you the particulars."

Several men nearby looked disappointed at not being privy to the information. Van licked his lips that had suddenly gone dry. Hours ago, he was in their shoes. He followed the chief to his office, where the man closed the door with a bang. "The walls have ears. Sit down, Toppel."

Every surface in the office was covered in paper, including the two guest chairs. After a moment's hesitation, Van gathered a stack from one of the chairs and set the pile on the floor. He sat down and raised his gaze to the chief seated behind the desk. "Ready, sir."

"Good. I would have selected you in the first place, but Riggs had some seniority. Sorry about the man's injury, but happy to have you on the team."

"Thank you." Van wiped his damp palms on his pants then laced his fingers. Would the man never get to the point?

"Here are your orders. Don't lose them, or you'll find yourself sent home, or to the brig. Too many of our kind are sneaking into places the military doesn't want us. Those behaviors have put us under a microscope. We need to get our stories, but getting in hot water with the authorities won't get us any points, and may get the whole industry banished. We can't risk that."

Van took the papers, scanned the documents, then folded and stuffed them into his breast coat pocket.

"The invasion is leaving from several locations on the Westminster and Dorset coasts, with Southampton and Portsmouth being the most important launch sites. We're talking thousands of ships and millions of troops. There are five landing sites in Normandy, with some sort of air strike planned as well, but we'll leave those boys alone. You'll accompany the infantry and armored divisions over on one of the transports and then wait on board until day two, after the guys have secured the beaches."

"I'm not able to off-load with them on D-day?"

"No. A couple of the photojournalists will go in with the first wave to capture the scenes, but I don't want you writers underfoot."

Disappointment warred with relief in Van's stomach. Waiting meant he wouldn't risk getting killed in the initial onslaught, but more importantly, if Cora was headed to Normandy, as he suspected, he'd be able to look for her. "Yes, sir."

"Make your way to Southampton and board with the Americans. Someone can help you find the right ships. Interview the boys. Get their stories. We want to personalize this invasion for our readers." The chief pulled out his pocket watch then frowned. He opened a drawer and extricated a wad of bills. "Launch is midnight tonight. Get there any way you can. And take this. Not sure how useful money will be, but it can't hurt."

Van gathered the funds and stood, tucking the bills into his wallet. "Sorry to hear about Riggs, but thanks for giving me this chance."

"Just keep your head down and come out of this alive." The chief's voice caught. "Godspeed."

Tears pricked the backs of Van's eyes. What would it be like to hold a position that required you to send someone into battle? To know that person might die? How did the commanders in the armed forces sleep at night? He shook his head. Too many questions.

He ducked out of the office and rushed from the building. Was public transportation too dicey? Would hitchhiking get him to the port in time? No. He'd save that as a last resort. First, a bus past the derailment, then he'd hop a train and hope for the best. *Lord, I know I don't deserve Your listening ear, but I'd appreciate some help getting to Southampton. And please keep Cora safe.*

His chest tightened. Where was she? Had she secured passage south, or was she stuck on the train somewhere? A chill slithered down his spine, and he stumbled. Or had she been injured or killed during the accident? He had to think she was still alive, or he couldn't function.

A bus rumbled toward him, and he trotted the last few yards to the stop. The doors popped open, and he waited for passengers to disembark before he boarded. "I need to get past Waterloo station. Any chance of that on this route?"

"Aye." The driver nodded. "That would be the Lambeth North stop, and we should be there in about thirty minutes. Will that do ya?"

"Yeah, thanks." Van lowered himself in the nearest vacant seat, pulled his fedora over his face, and closed his eyes. Cora would tell him that God was working out his path, allowing the accident to get him back to Broadcasting House and the subsequent assignment. *Is that what's happening here, God? I'm trying to have more faith, but…well…You know how much I'm struggling.* He sighed and tried to shut out the murmured conversations. Over four years in England, and he still hadn't acclimated to the constant noise.

The vehicle bumped over the uneven macadam, stopping every few blocks for passengers. Miles passed. Another stop. Another.

"Hey, mister. This is your stop."

Van opened his eyes and pushed up his hat over his forehead. "Thanks." He rose and swung himself out of the bus then crossed the street to the Tube station. Only a fraction of the way to the port, and he was already tired from travel. Cobbling together the trip was tedious at best and exhausting at its worst. He'd be wrung out by the time he arrived, but the boys in uniform had it worse.

Two hours later, he jumped from the train and walked out of the station. The streets were jammed with military vehicles and soldiers. The rumble of engines mingled with shouts and whistles from the men. Horns blared.

Hoisting his satchel over his shoulder, he weaved through the traffic and hastened toward the docks. His heart pounded, and his gaze ricocheted from face to face. Was Cora here? Or had he followed a faulty leap in logic? Was he headed to Normandy and possible death just for a story?

Chapter Twenty-Eight

Shoulder to shoulder with soldiers, Red Cross girls, medics, and army nurses on the rolling deck of the hospital ship, Cora took a deep breath to steady herself. Her heart beat in her ears, adding to the cacophony of noise that enveloped her.

Officers shouted orders. Equipment clanged. Hatches slammed. Planes roared overhead. The periodic rat-a-tat-tat of machine-gun fire in the distance sliced the air. The ship pitched in the choppy seas. It was no secret that Eisenhower had hoped for better weather for the invasion. Had yesterday's assault gone better or worse than planned?

The crowd thinned as more and more of them went over the rail and down the rope ladder to the waiting boats that would take them to shore. Cora's hands slicked at the thought of dangling on the side of the ship sixty feet above the water. They hadn't lost anyone into the cold, frothing ocean, but there was always a first time. She shivered. Get ahold of yourself, girl. You're here now. It's what you wanted.

She straightened her spine, and the ship swayed. Off-balance, she bumped the medic at her side and tromped on his foot. Her face heated. "Sorry."

"No problem, girlie. Sardines have more room that we do." He stuck out his hand. "Mitch Gaynor from Iowa. Come here often?" He winked and laughed as if he'd cracked the funniest joke in the world.

"Cora Strealer from New Hampshire." Her heart skipped a beat. The man was from Iowa. Like Van. She sighed and tugged at her baggy fatigues. What would he think about her stunt?

About halfway across the Channel, she'd risked emerging from closets and bathrooms. No one had questioned her presence, and she blended in with the other women. Claiming she'd lost her bag, she secured an olive drab uniform and boots. The pants and jacket were decidedly more comfortable than the ill-fitting Red Cross skirt and blouse. The boots were too big and had already rubbed blisters on both heels.

Mitch jabbed her with his elbow and pointed to the distant beach. Littered with vehicles, cannons, corpses, and crates, the sandy stretch of land was nothing like the resorts along the lake at home. Her stomach roiled, and she swallowed against the bile that burned her throat. She squeezed her eyes closed.

"Hey, you okay?" Mitch's voice came close to her ear.

She jumped, and her eyes flew open. "Uh, yeah. A bit overwhelmed, that's all. This day will be etched on my memory for the rest of my life."

"Amen, sister. I've survived a bunch of campaigns, but none this big. There must be a half million boys here. Who of us will remain by the end of this little party?"

"They're so young, aren't they? Barely out of high school, most of them."

"You say that as if you are a wizened, old woman." He rubbed his jaw and made a show of studying her face. "You can't be a day over twenty-five."

A guffaw burst from her lips, and she covered her mouth. "I've already crested thirty, my friend, and then some. But thanks for the compliment."

"All right, ladies and gents. We're ready for the next wave. Step lively, so we can get this tub filled and on its way."

Cora licked her lips that had suddenly gone dry. She pressed her hand against her middle. "This is me. See you on the other side?"

"You can be sure of it. I'll watch your six."

She inched forward, pressed in from all sides. One by one, her fellow passengers crawled over the rail then disappeared from sight.

"You're up, sister. Grip the railing, sling your leg over the side, and put your foot on the rung. The rope will give a little, but don't panic. Move one hand from the ship to the rung, then the next. At that point you can make your way down the side. Just like a monkey at the zoo."

Her body trembled. "Except the monkey isn't smart enough to know he can get hurt."

"You'll be fine. At this point, there are so many people in the transport, they'll break your fall."

"Reassuring, sailor."

He shrugged and swept his arm toward the rail. "M'lady. Your chariot awaits."

With a grip on the rail, she followed the young man's directions and was soon clinging to the knotted ladder. The hemp scraped her palms as she descended. Encouragement floated up from below. She could do this.

The ship rolled toward her, and she swung away from the side. Seconds later, the ship leaned the other direction, and she slammed into the hull with a bang. Her grip loosened, and she flailed her arm, grabbing at the moving cable. Her breath came in ragged gasps. Fingers searching…reaching, then coiling around the rope. *Thank You, Father.*

Her vision swirled as dizziness threatened to overtake her. Breathe in. Breathe out. Her vision cleared, and she extended her leg, her boot finding a foothold. Cheers erupted, and she grimaced. More like a sloth than a monkey, she made her way to the bottom of the ladder, finally landing in the boat, its engine vibrating the crowded watercraft.

Heart banging in her chest, she took her place next to some nurses. The redheaded gal from Maine, who she met at breakfast, squeezed her arm. "You did great."

Cora rolled her eyes. "Nice of you to say, but I'm trying not to think about how I'm going to get back on board."

"One thing at a time." She smiled. "Haven't you scaled trees back home in New Hampshire?"

"Not if I could help it." Cora laughed. "I left that to my youngest sister. She's fearless."

"You are too. Don't forget that."

Twenty minutes later, the boat was filled to capacity, and one of the men steered it toward shore. Dipping and weaving, the craft bucked and jerked, fighting the waves. Men and women moaned.

"This is worse than the ship," a voice complained. "How about if I swim to the beach?"

Someone coughed then threw up over the side. The wind wafted the acrid smell toward Cora, who gasped and pinched her nose. Breathing through her mouth wasn't much better.

Murmuring rose, and someone else was sick.

"This was not in the brochure."

Laughter relieved the tension, and Cora smiled. She recognized Mitch's voice. No wonder he was a medic. Able to put people at ease in the worst situations. Much like she'd seen Van do.

Van. Where was he?

The boat continued to lumber toward the beach. Pressed against the side, she scanned the activity. Men scrambled across the dunes then dove behind whatever they could find that provided protection from the occasional crack of gunfire. Smoke and dust hung above the landing site.

"Okay, folks. This is as close as we get." A man with captain's bars pointed to a cadre of small boats bobbing near the beach. "Your job is to wade ashore, pick up casualties, and get them onto those craft which will ferry them to us. You're familiar with triage protocols. Send us the worst cases first. Be careful. Our boys haven't cleared out all the machine-gun nests yet. Don't take unnecessary risks."

"Yes, sir," Cora and her shipmates responded in unison.

Two men at the front dropped the ramp with a splash. Water sloshed over the metal gangway as the passengers scrambled off the boat and into the ocean. Minutes later, Cora was in the churning sea. She kicked her legs, pointing her toes until she found purchase.

The briny air mingled with the smell of gunpowder and fuel. At least the fetid stink of vomit no longer filled her nose. Up to her chin in the water, Cora pushed herself forward. Discarded and lost items bobbed on the surface. She stumbled and submerged, then propelled herself upward. Coughing, she wiped the water from her eyes.

A haze hung over the scene that seemed unreal as if she were watching a newsreel, except in color. The water became shallower as she got closer to shore. Finally, lapping at her ankles, it foamed at her feet.

She bent over, hands on her knees, and took several deep breaths. She'd made it. Pride filled her, then guilt. How many hadn't survived?

"All right, Strealer. Break time is over." Mitch clapped her on the back. "How about if you work with me?"

Straightening, she turned and curled her lip in a mock sneer. "What if I'd rather work with someone else?"

He grinned.

She smiled in reply. "Guess that's not going to happen."

"No." He settled his steel helmet on his head. "But good try on your part." He gestured to the western end of the beach. "Let's start there, and make our way toward that cluster of boats."

She nodded and followed him to the far end of the coastline, averting her eyes from the stiff, twisted forms that lay half-buried in the sand. There was nothing she could do for the men, and graves registration would take care of them. She shuddered at the memory of her discovery that each person carried his or her own canvas body bag. A practical, necessary evil.

"Help me," the plaintive cry of a wounded man came from behind a crate.

"Mitch, over here." Cora hurried across the sand, her feet stumbling and bumbling over the debris. She ducked behind the crate and gasped. Her stomach roiled. A young man, who looked barely old enough to shave, was propped against the wooden box. Crusted with blood, his uniform was more rusty-brown than green. He pressed his hand against a bleeding wound in his belly.

She pressed her lips together and swayed. What had she been thinking to come here? Her idea to cover the invasion now seemed cavalier and foolish. She'd figured to show up, grab some interviews and descriptions, and write compelling stories. Perhaps the upper echelon was smart in forbidding nonmedical women in a combat zone. The stories would be compelling, all right, but would she have the fortitude to write them?

Mitch yanked on her arm, and she fell onto her knees. "Sorry."

"Don't apologize. The first hundred times are the worst. I won't say you'll get used to it, but a certain amount of numbness will overtake you."

"Okay." Her voice trembled in her ears.

"Stomach wound puts this guy almost at the top of the list." Mitch opened his medkit and pulled out a container of sulfa and some bandages. He moved the soldier's hand away from his wound and shook the medicine over the man's middle. With swift motions that spoke of the countless times he'd performed the action, Mitch bound the youngster's injury. He patted the man's shoulder. "Someone will be by to put you on a stretcher and take you to the ship. You're done for a while, son."

"Thank you, sir."

"Would you like me to pray with you?"

Cora's eyes shot open. Mitch was a believer. Had God paired her with him on purpose?

"Yes, please."

Hand still on the man, Mitch bowed his head and murmured a quiet prayer that she couldn't hear, but his gracious, confident tone bolstered her lagging spirit.

"Amen. God bless you, son." Mitch stuffed the sulfa container and unused bandages into his kit and climbed to his feet. "Next patient."

"Right."

They staggered along the beach, stopping and administering aid to each injured man. Cora lost track of time. At some point, the sun reached its zenith then headed for the horizon. Twice, she and Mitch had wolfed down some C-rations before continuing their mission. Mouth dry, her tongue stuck to the roof of her mouth. Her hair stuck to the sides of her face, and her uniform was crusty with blood and dried saltwater. Her heels burned with each step as her boots rubbed her blisters raw.

Was this what the attack and aftermath had been like at Pearl? Only worse? Had Brian heard the whistle of bombs and the snap of gunfire before he died? Did he experience terror in his last moments on earth? Or did the ship explode in an instant taking him with no awareness or pain?

Her lips trembled, and she pressed them together. Tending the injured and ill had reopened her own wound of grief. As if she were losing Brian again. Losing the possibility of what they could have had as a married couple if he'd lived.

Van's face wavered in her mind. Where was he? She had a chance at something and threw it away by running off in a hair-brained scheme to best her news colleagues. Even Myrtle hadn't been stupid enough to board a ship. Not that Van could keep her from harm, only God could do that, but she'd feel a lot safer by his side.

Dear Father, please keep me safe. Forgive my subterfuge and conniving to go where I shouldn't. I don't deserve Your mercy. I know that, but please allow me to survive this day…and the rest of the days

A blanket of peace settled on her shoulders, and her muscles sagged. A smile tugged at her lips. Regardless of how God chose to answer her prayer, she was prepared to face the day. If only Van were here to share the experience.

Chapter Twenty-Nine

Van looked over his shoulder as he slogged through the knee-high water toward the shore. Like industrious ants at a picnic, men swarmed the beach, and everyone seemed to have a job. What had it taken to coordinate the logistics of the yesterday's invasion?

Gunfire crackled, and he hurled himself behind a stack of crates. The lieutenant had warned them about pockets of Germans still hiding in the hills above, but the reality of being shot at was more frightening than Van imagined. How did these young men force themselves to keep moving forward into the danger?

A short, wiry soldier approached. "I wouldn't worry about getting shot, sir. You never hear the one meant for you."

"Okaaay." Van gulped. He needed to man up. Huddling behind matériel wouldn't do anyone any good. "What can I do to help?"

The man gestured to a group of medics who moved between the men, stopping to provide aid and comfort. "Those boys always need assistance, or you can carry stretchers to the transport boats."

"Got it. Uh, thanks."

"No problem, sir." The soldier touched two fingers to his helmet in a farewell salute. "Good luck to you."

"And you." Van watched him zigzag across the sand, hands wrapped around his rifle, head ducked between his shoulders. With a deep breath, he climbed to his feet and mimicked the soldier's side-to-side dash along the beach. Perspiration broke out at his hairline, and his shirt stuck to his back despite the chill in the air. The dust that clung to the air clogged his throat, and he coughed. Oh, for the clean, crisp air of Iowa.

He came alongside a pair of medics bent over a soldier who bled from several places. Face scrunched in pain, his breathing was loud and ragged. With swift motions, they cleaned and bandaged the young man, then gave him some morphine. One of the corpsmen leaned close to the injured soldier. "You'll be fine, but the wait to get on board may be a while, so be patient."

Eyes closed, the patient nodded.

The medics rose and glanced at Van. The shorter of the two men said, "What can we do for you, sir?"

"Uh, I was going to ask you the same question. I have no medical training, and I'm here as a correspondent, but there must be something I can do other than take up space."

"Appreciate the offer, sir." He gestured to the line of stretchers filled with injured, moaning soldiers. "How about if you get those men on board? Doesn't take any amount of training to lift one end of the litter and carry it."

"Perfect. Much obliged."

"No, thank you, sir." He nodded to his partner, and they moved to the next groaning soldier lying on the sand.

Van trotted to a corpsman who seemed to be in charge of the stretcher bearers. He waited for the man to look in his direction before he spoke. "I'm here to help get the wounded onto the boats."

A frown creasing his forehead, the medic cocked his head. "Aren't you one of the press guys?"

"Yes, but I'm fairly certain that trying to secure interviews right now isn't the best use of my time." He sent the man a conciliatory smile. "I'd like to be put to use, and one of your men suggested this job might be a fit for me."

After a long stare as if he were weighing Van's words and motives, the medic gave him a curt nod. "Fine. Start at the end closest to the boats. The men have been put in order of seriousness of their injuries. Watch what you're doing. Try not to shake the stretcher. Firm and steady is what you want." He looked past Van. "Meyerson. This guy's with you."

"Yes, sir!" A burly soldier with hands the size of catcher's mitts lumbered toward him.

"Van Toppel, United Press-turned-stretcher-bearer."

Meyerson grinned. "Be sure to get my name in the paper."

"Absolutely." Van returned his smile.

Together, they lifted the first litter, and Van's eyes widened. He recognized the ashen face of the soldier. The young man had been one of the first to greet him when he boarded. They'd shared a meal and spoken of their respective hometowns, miles apart in distance, but nearly identical in their small town-sameness. "Beasley, I told you to duck."

The boy's eyes fluttered. "I tried, sir, but I wasn't fast enough." He grimaced and moaned.

Van's heart tugged. "Hang tight. We'll get you aboard, and you'll be at the hospital in no time."

"Caton didn't make it." Beasley's voice cracked. "He was right next to me. One minute we were joking that the next time we were on a beach we wanted lots of pretty girls with us, and the next we were being shot at, and he dropped like a stone. Bullet caught him in the neck. He was gone in an instant."

"Try not to talk, Beasley. You need to rest."

Beasley nodded, and a tear slipped from his eye and ran down the side of his head.

Hands gripping the poles on the stretcher, Van marched toward the fleet of boats that huddled near the shore. Planes roared overheard, and jeeps rumbled across the sand. Men barked orders while others shouted warnings. The acrid smell of gunpowder clung to the air.

He huffed and puffed, his feet struggling to remain steady in the shifting sand. He snorted a dry laugh. He was in his own version of the Bible story about the man who built his house on rock and his friend who built on sand. Memories of his grandmother washed over him. While he was a child, she'd sit beside him on the bed and tell him a different story each night before they prayed. The story hadn't meant much to him, and as an adult he hadn't given it a lot of thought.

Yes, he was a believer, and he read his Bible, but he hadn't studied the Book. Amazing how God was using his horrific experiences of the day to draw him back. God's heart must be breaking to watch the evil that sought to overtake the world, and the loss of so many young men and women, on both sides of the conflict.

"This way, sir."

The voice broke his musings, and he nodded to the man pointing to one of the craft. Van grunted as he hefted his end of the stretcher above the water. He waded into the ocean to the side of the boat. Two men reached over the hull and wrestled the litter into the craft, muscles bulging under their filthy fatigues.

His muscles, on the other hand, trembled and cramped. As a desk jockey, he exercised very little. *Please, God, give me strength for the tasks. I don't want to let these guys down.*

He and Meyerson returned to the line of stretchers and lifted another patient. Back to the boat. Back to the wounded. Hours passed during which, at some point, he'd stopped flinching at the sound of bullets. He kept his eyes riveted to his partner's back as they trundled toward the transports then on the line of stretchers during his return trip. If he made the mistake of letting his gaze scan the beach, his heart would burst with grief at the sight of so many dead soldiers.

Young men whose lives were cut short, their potential extinguished like a bucket of water on a flame. Just because some madman thought he should rule the world. *Dear Father, save us all.*

The sun dipped low in the sky, its orange, pink, and violet rays spreading across the water and the sandy coastline. A salty breeze lifted his hair and stroked his cheek. Before coming to Europe he'd never seen the ocean. After the war, would he be able to look at the sea without thinking about today and the days that followed?

"Take a break, sir. Some of the guys have rustled up dinner, well, a passel of C-rations that claim to be a meal."

Van chuckled and rotated his neck in an effort to unknot the muscles in his shoulders. No dice. His body still ached with occasional shards of pain that shot down his back. He'd managed to keep up with his younger counterpart. His stomach rumbled in anticipation of the food. No matter that it came from a tin and contained very little flavor.

He hunkered on the ground next to Meyerson and accepted a can from one of the other men. Dirty from head to toe, exhaustion lined their faces. No one spoke, instead wolfing down the contents of the government-issued food as if it were haute cuisine. Moments later, belly full, he rose to give an approaching soldier his spot.

Eyes burning from the gritty dust, Van blinked trying to persuade moisture to materialize. No luck. He sighed and wandered away from the group then froze.

Cora?

Or was his imagination playing tricks on him. Was his exhaustion conjuring up the woman he'd grown to love over the few months they'd had together?

He squinted against the sun's glare.

About fifty yards away, and shoulder to shoulder with a medic, the petite blonde woman bent over a wounded man. Face white under the grime, and dark smudges below her haunted blue eyes, she bandaged a soldier's leg while her colleague worked on the soldier's head. She cocked her head and caught her teeth in her lower lip. His heart leapt. It was Cora.

Tears sprang to his eyes, the long-awaited lubricant a result of her presence. His knees wavered, and he swayed, nearly falling to the ground.

"You okay, sir?"

Van tore away his gaze and looked at Meyerson who repeated the question. Concern etched on his face, he gripped Van's arm. "You look like you're going into shock. Sit down before you fall down."

"No. I need to go, but I'll be back. I promise."

"You don't have to, sir. You've worked like a yeoman today. We appreciate the help, but we'll be fine. Get along with you. There will be plenty to do tomorrow if you still have a mind to give us a hand."

"If I can be here, I will. Count on it."

"Thank you, sir."

Meyerson headed back to the group, and Van wheeled around, his feet fumbling to gain traction in the sand.

"Cora!"

Raspy, his hoarse words barely sounded above the roar of the engines that permeated the landing site. He waved his arms and ran toward her, stumbling and awkward as a newborn colt.

Forty yards.

Thirty yards.

Twenty yards.

Ten yards.

He stopped. "Cora!"

Her head shot up and whipped around toward him. Her eyes widened, and her jaw dropped, forming her mouth into a perfect O. Her hands stilled over the patient, then she seemed to remember what she was doing, and finished bandaging the leg.

Van's heart banged in his chest and thundered in his ears. Was she pleased to see him? Would she be upset? Why was he suddenly so unsure about her?

Cora said something to the medic, and the man glanced at Van then nodded before turning his attention back to the wounded soldier. She staggered to her feet and stood in place, uncertainty darkening her eyes.

Stomach vibrating as if a pair of squirrel was dancing the Charleston, he rushed forward. She was alive and uninjured. Doing her part to provide aid and comfort to the men in the aftermath of battle despite the horrific scenes that played out before her. His brave, stalwart girl.

She walked toward him, her steps slow and tentative. "Van, what are you doing here? Did you disobey orders, too?"

"No. Riggs was injured in a train accident. He's going to be okay but was in no condition to travel to a battle zone, so I was selected as his replacement." He shrugged. "I was headed here anyway after I figured this is where you'd gone."

"Were you going to try to stop me?" She frowned. "I had to come."

"I know you did, but I was afraid for you." Arms outstretched, he closed the distance between them. "I thought to prevent you from going then maybe to just keep you safe."

"Van, we've talked about this. I appreciate what you're trying to do, but I have to make my own way without anyone's help…your help. To write stories that inform the people from a woman's point of view. To write stories that show I'm a serious journalist. And to do that I have to be alone."

"But–"

"Ow!" Cora reached for her leg and crumpled to the ground. Her face white and lined with pain, she moaned. "I've been shot."

Chapter Thirty

Burning, searing pain shot up Cora's leg. Van's face swam in front of her eyes as she fought for consciousness. Not a life-threatening injury, but one unlike anything she'd ever experienced. She gritted her teeth against the desire to cry out. Men with more serious wounds should be allowed to wail and groan, but not her. She would make Van proud of her bravery. Traitorous, hot tears poured from her eyes.

"Medic! Over here." On his knees, Van gripped her hand and brushed her hair away from her face, his hands warm and soft against her skin. Should she allow the darkness to take her? If she was unconscious, she wouldn't feel the agony.

"Stay with me, Cora. You're going to be fine." He leaned close to her ear. "My strong, spunky girl. Bullets can't stop you."

She tried to laugh, but the effort sounded more like a strangled gurgle. "I'm not strong. I'm afraid." She spoke through stiff lips. "This is God's way of punishing me for breaking the rules. I deserve this."

"No, this isn't God. He's watching over you and will see you through. This is a German soldier following orders." His shoulders slumped. "Your injury is my fault. I stood in the middle of a war zone as if we were in the park."

"Enough talking. Let's get her behind that jeep." The medic wrapped his arm around her, and Van supported her on the other side. They carried her between them, and then laid her on the ground, protected from the fighting. The corpsman dropped beside Cora and opened his kit. He pulled out scissors, sulfa, and bandages. "I'll try to be gentle, but brace yourself."

Eyes closed, she nodded.

The sound of ripping as he cut away her pant leg. Fingers pressing, probing the injured area. She grunted and fisted her hands against the knives of pain.

"Excellent. There is an exit wound, which means the bullet went all the way through. No one will have to dig for it." He cleaned her leg, then shook sulfa over the damaged leg and bound the wound. "You may be a while getting onto a transport, but you should be fine." The medic patted her shoulder. "Some people will do anything to get out of a little work." Humor laced his voice.

"Yeah, that's what this is." She opened her eyes and grimaced, reaching for his hand. "It was a pleasure to work with you. Thanks for letting me tag along."

"Anytime, Miss Strealer. One of my best partners." He climbed to his feet. "Look after our girl."

"Of course."

Cora blew out a deep breath. "Well, this wasn't how I planned to cover the invasion."

"You can call the column View from the Stretcher."

"How about Strealer on a Stretcher."

"I like my title better."

Pushing herself up with her elbows, she shook her head. "We can argue about the title all we want, but we can't assume I'll have a column to go back to. A couple of hours ago, I ran into a major who knew me from London. He said, in no uncertain terms, that he'd ensure my credentials were revoked for being in a combat zone and impersonating a Red Cross worker. I guess I deserve that consequence."

He shifted so that he sat next to her then draped his arm around her back, bracing her against himself. "I'm sorry if you lose your accreditation. Women not being allowed to cover all aspects of the war isn't fair. You're just as much of a journalist as any guy out there."

"That opinion is downright progressive, *Mr. Toppel*." She stared at him. He *had* changed.

"Thank you, *Miss Strealer*." He cleared his throat. "Kidding aside, I have changed. While terrified you might be killed, I realized that no matter what I did…or do…I can't ever keep you safe. Only God can take care of you…protect you." He raked his fingers through his hair and blew out a loud breath. "You have to follow His leading, and if that means putting yourself in danger, I have to trust you to Him and His perfect will."

Her leg throbbed, but the shards of shooting pain had dissipated. Perhaps she'd make it out of Normandy alive after all. Her face heated, and she ducked her head. "Which I haven't been doing. I'm here because I wanted to prove something to myself and the rest of the world, not because I felt God leading me. I broke rules to get here. That's not the kind of behavior He expects from His children. I'm not a shining example of being a believer for that major or anyone."

He rubbed lazy circles on her back. "We all mess up, and I, of all people, understand what you did. I've been pushing and shoving my way up the ranks, too."

Tingles raced up and down her spine at the warmth of his hand through her jacket. Was he comforting her as a friend and colleague, or did he feel the electricity between them? Had she ruined the opportunity for more than a friendship? A sigh escaped, and she pressed her lips together.

"Are you in pain? You should be resting, and I'm yammering on and on as if we're at a picnic."

"The leg is sore and aches a bit, but isn't unbearable." Her chin trembled. "My emotions seem to be running amok. Perhaps the military is right in their rules for women."

"You've been shot. I'd say you have a right to your emotions. And as for the military and its rules, well…that remains to be seen." He stroked her jaw then cupped her cheek. "Listen, I need to tell you something. Please promise you'll hear me out without interrupting."

Heart pounding, she leaned into his hand. "Okay."

"Somehow I pictured this exchange a little differently." A wry smile curved his lips. "I love you, Cora."

She gasped, and he pressed his index finger against her mouth.

"Somewhere in the midst of this chaos, I fell in love with you. I've never felt like this about anyone. You challenge me, encourage me, and exasperate me, but you fill me like nothing else has ever done, and I can't imagine my life without you. I want to be your partner in more than just the news industry. Please say you'll marry me, and we can spend a lifetime exploring the world or just one corner of it, if you prefer."

Mouth working, Cora struggled to put her thoughts into words. She'd vowed never to remarry, and certainly not in wartime. Was she being foolish? Short-sighted? Disloyal to Brian, whose image grew dimmer with each passing day?

Separated more than they were together during the short marriage, they barely knew each other. Their relationship had been sweet, but immature, a fledgling kind of love that was untried, unproven, and then it was too late. Brian was gone. But now, God was giving her a second chance.

"Please, Cora, talk to me. Tell me you love me, too. That I'm not imagining the connection we have."

Laughter bubbled up from inside, and she nodded. "I've been fighting the feeling because I was afraid. Afraid to open up my heart again. Afraid I was being unfaithful to Brian's memory. Just...afraid."

A wrinkled creased his brow. "And now?" His words were whispered, uncertain.

"Now, I'm not." She sighed. "All of my preconceived notions seem silly. I don't know why I let them–"

He pressed his mouth to hers, cutting off further conversation. Gentle at first, then more insistent, his kiss explored her lips. Then he pulled away and kissed the tip of her nose. His eyes sparkled. "You didn't answer my question."

"You interrupted me." She giggled and tapped a finger on her cheek, looking off in the distance, pretending to consider his proposal. "My answer is…yes."

With a shout, he pulled her to him, then sprang back. "Did I hurt you?"

"No, you've healed the hurt that was crippling me, and I love you more than you can imagine." She snaked her arms around his neck and laid her head on his chest, the steady beat of his heart thrumming in rhythm with hers.

THE END

Historical Notes

I enjoy the opportunity to insert historical figures into my stories. *The Widow & The War Correspondent* features three real people who lived and served during WWII:

Winston Churchill: Born of an American mother and British father, Churchill became prime minister after a call for division (effectively a vote of no confidence) in Neville Chamberlain's government. He joined the British Army at the age of 21 and saw action in British India, the Anglo-Sudan War, and the Second Boer War. He wrote books about his campaigns and earned fame as a war correspondent. He became an MP (Member of Parliament) at 25 years of age. During World War I, he rejoined the military and was appointed commander of the 6th Battalion, Royal Scots Fusiliers.

Martha Gellhorn: One of the 127 certified female war correspondents during World War II. Born in 1908, she became aware of civic issues early on: participating in a women's suffrage rally at the tender age of eight years old. She left college to begin her career as a journalist with her first published articles appearing in *The New Republic*. A desire to become a foreign correspondent took her to Paris with the United Press. Gellhorn had a close friendship with Eleanor Roosevelt and lived in the White House during the early years of FDR's presidency helping the First Lady write her "My Day" column. She met author Ernest Hemingway in 1936, and the couple traveled to Spain where she covered the Spanish Civil War. She traveled to Europe in the spring of 1938 and reported the war from such locations as Finland, Hong Kong, Burma, Singapore, and England. Because women were not allowed in combat zones, she did not have the credentials to accompany the troops to the Normandy landings.

Undeterred, Gellhorn hid in a hospital ship bathroom, and upon landing impersonated a stretcher bearer. I have no proof of when Gellhorn was in England when Cora was, but I don't have proof that she wasn't either!

Rita Hayworth: Born Margarita Carmen Cansino in Brooklyn, New York, Rita got her start dancing. (Her mother danced with the Ziegfield Follies, and her grandfather was a famous classical Spanish dancer.) After being seen by a movie executive while dancing at a club in Hollywood, she signed on with Fox Film Corporation at the age of 16. She eventually moved to Columbia Pictures where she changed her name to Rita Hayworth because her image was "too Mediterranean." A popular pin-up girl, Hayworth did extensive service during World War II, from donating the bumpers from her car for scrap to volunteering at the Hollywood Canteen where she served food and danced with servicemen. She also volunteered in the Naval Aid Auxiliary and traveled thousands of miles conducting war bond rallies.

What did you think of _The Widow & The War Correspondent?_

Thank you so much for purchasing _The Widow & The War Correspondent_. You could have selected any number of books to read, but you chose this book.

I hope it added encouragement and exhortation to your life. If so, it would be nice if you could share this book with your family and friends by posting to Facebook (www.facebook.com) and/or Twitter (www.twitter.com).

If you enjoyed this book and found some benefit in reading it, I'd appreciate it if you could take some time to post a review on Amazon, Goodreads, Kobo, GooglePlay, Apple Books, or other book review site of your choice. Your feedback and support will help me to improve my writing craft for future projects and make this book even better.

Thank you again for your purchase.

Blessings,

Linda Shenton Matchett

Acknowledgments

Although writing a book is a solitary task, it is not a solitary journey. There have been many who have helped and encouraged me along the way.

My parents, Richard and Jean Shenton, who presented me with my first writing tablet and encouraged me to capture my imagination with words. Thanks, Mom and Dad!

Scribes212 – my ACFW online critique group: Valerie Goree, Marcia Lahti, and the late Loretta Boyett (passed on to Glory, but never forgotten). Without your input, my writing would not be nearly as effective.

Eva Marie Everson – my mentor/instructor with Christian Writers' Guild. You took a timid, untrained student and turned her into a writer. Many thanks!

SincNE, and the folks who coordinate the Crimebake Writing Conference. I have attended many writing conferences, but without a doubt, Crimebake is one of the best. The workshops, seminars, panels, critiques, and every tiny aspect are well-executed, professional, and educational.

Special thanks to Hank Phillippi Ryan, Halle Ephron, and Roberta Isleib for your encouragement and spot-on critiques of my work.

Thanks to my Book Brigade who provide information, encouragement, and support.

Paula Proofreader (https://paulaproofreader.wixsite.com/home): I'm so glad I found you! My work is cleaner because of your eagle eye. Any mistakes are completely mine.

A heartfelt thank you to my brothers, Jack Shenton and Douglas Shenton, and my sister, Susan Shenton Greger for being enthusiastic cheerleaders during my writing journey. Your support means more than you'll know.

My husband, Wes, deserves special kudos for understanding my need to write. Thank you for creating my writing room – it's perfect, and I'm thankful for it every day. Thank you for your willingness to accept a house that's a bit cluttered, laundry that's not always done, and meals on the go. I love you.

And finally, to God be the glory. I thank Him for giving me the gift of writing and the inspiration to tell stories that shine the light on His goodness and mercy.

Read on for the first chapter in *Love's Harvest*, book one in the "Wartime Brides" series.

Volga Region, Russia, 1923

Chapter One

"We'll die if we don't leave this place. Pack only what you can carry." Edmund Hirsch poked his bony arms into the sleeves of his wool coat that sported more holes than Swiss cheese. A paroxysm of coughing gripped his body, the result of a mustard gas attack on his German platoon nine years ago during The Great War.

After several minutes the coughing ceased, and he mopped the sweat from his forehead with a dingy, gray handkerchief. "Be ready. We set out tomorrow at first light."

"Where will we go, *Vati*?" Five-year-old Conrad's voice trembled.

"Don't be a baby, Conrad." Older by two minutes, Conrad's twin brother, Manfred, finished tying his boot laces and jumped off the chair, his shoes clomping against the bare wood floor. His bright blue eyes blazed above his hollow cheeks.

"Hush, children." Noreen stroked Conrad's white-blond hair and met her husband's terse look with one of her own. "You heard your father. There's no time to waste."

Noreen yanked the zipper closed on her over-stuffed canvas satchel. Always resourceful, Edmund had attached straps to the moss-green bag so she could wear it on her back. She would also carry a suitcase in each hand. The journey promised to be arduous.

Sighing, she wiped a weary hand across her dry eyes. Even if she had any tears remaining, crying was useless. It would not make their situation less dire.

Muted voices and the occasional bump filtered through the ceiling from the boys' bedroom above. Noreen shivered and hunched into her threadbare, ruby-red sweater. An impulse purchase made during her honeymoon, the garment held more memories than warmth. Edmund insisted it brought out the roses in her cheeks.

She tossed the bulging satchel to the floor and turned her attention to the yawning luggage on the bed. Two steel pots and a fry pan nestled in the bottom of one boxy, brown suitcase between faded blue towels that had been a belated wedding present from her mother and father.

Hopefully, Edmund would find somewhere they could live in his home country with enough food to actually cook. Here, along the Volga River in Russia, the crops had failed again, and the famine was entering its second year. The decision whether to eat or plant their seed wheat had caused many families to die of starvation.

Shuffling footsteps sounded behind her. She turned as Edmund enveloped her in his arms. Nestling against his too-thin chest, she breathed in his musky scent. He bent and kissed her forehead, his black beard scraping her skin.

"You work too hard." He tucked a stray strand of her nutmeg-colored hair behind her ear.

She leaned into his touch. "Isn't that why you married me?"

"No, *Schatzi,* it is most certainly not." He grinned. "You stole my heart. I had to marry you, or I would die a broken man."

"Don't joke about that. Our friends are dying every day." She frowned. "Who knew this famine would last so long? If it weren't for the bit of help arriving from America's Volga Relief Society, matters would be much worse."

"They are sending more assistance than we are receiving. Jakob told me there is proof the government is confiscating some of the packages and keeping the money to construct new buildings and conduct repairs. As always, development of the country is valued above the lives of the people."

"Shhh!" She pressed the work-worn fingers of her right hand against his lips. "You could get in trouble for saying that. Then where would we be?"

Edmund hugged her. "There is no one to hear us, but I understand your fear. Many unexplained disappearances make for extreme caution." He released her and gestured toward the pile of clothes on their bed. "Enough depressing talk. What can I do to help?"

"Do you have our passports? With the government ratcheting up the price, we have no more savings to purchase new ones."

"Now who's speaking out against the authorities?" He patted the breast pocket of his coat. "I have the passports and our traveling papers safe and sound."

"Good." Noreen waved him away. "Then go see what the boys are about. I gave explicit instructions about what to pack, but they have a mind of their own." She shook her head. "Well, Manfred does. Conrad simply tags along."

He kissed the tip of her nose and raised his hand in mock salute. "*Jawohl!*"

She giggled and pushed him out of the room. Closing the door behind him, she sobered and dropped to her knees next to the bed. "Dear Heavenly Father, thank You for Edmund. He is a good man. Give him strength for the journey and keep us safe as we travel. Soften the hearts of his family so they will welcome us home."

Home.

Berlin was Edmund's home. Not hers.

English born and bred, Noreen stroked the floral bedspread as visions of daffodils in Regents Park flitted through her head, their golden yellow blooms swaying in the breeze. Big Ben soaring into the sky. Tower Bridge spanning the River Thames. Pristine white swans fishing the waters of Serpentine Lake in Hyde Park where a chance meeting changed the trajectory of her life.

In an effort to heal his damaged lungs, Edmund moved to London after the war. Someone told him the damp English air would act as a balm. A lover of art, he had attended the Spring Festival where she sat under a tent selling her baskets.

She climbed to her feet, and her gaze sought out the willow basket on their dresser. The basket Edmund purchased when he returned to her booth after taking his girlfriend home. His last date with the woman.

Noreen's smile broadened. Who knew basket weaving would catch her a husband? She flushed as she remembered the conversation.

"If I purchase this basket, will you go out with me?"

"What about your girlfriend?"

"I told her we were finished, that I was going to marry you."

"Isn't that a bit rash? You don't even know me."

"I know enough."

After a whirlwind courtship, Edmund asked for her hand in marriage. Her parents objected, so Edmund took her to the register office where he wed her in front of two gray-haired, bored-looking clerks. A year later the twins were born, and her parents decided being grandparents was more important than holding a grudge. They eventually grew to love their German son-in-law as much as their daughter did. Enough to support the family's move to Russia in another effort to heal Edmund's lungs. She swallowed against the lump in her throat. Her parents' death last year in a train accident still stung.

Overheard, a thump followed by laughter broke her reverie. Warmth filled her. She loved her country, but she loved Edmund more. That is why she would leave all but her most necessary possessions and travel to yet another foreign country to live with her in-laws. People she had never met who spoke a language she didn't know.

Other Titles

Romance

Love's Harvest, Wartime Brides, Book 1

Love's Rescue, Wartime Brides, Book 2

Love's Belief, Wartime Brides, Book 3

Love's Allegiance, Wartime Brides, Book 4

Love Found in Sherwood Forest

A Love Not Forgotten

On the Rails

A Doctor in the House (The Hope of Christmas Collection)

Spies & Sweethearts, Sisters in Service, Book 1

The Mechanic & the MD, Sisters in Service, Book 2

The Widow & the War Correspondent, Sisters in Service, Book 3

Mystery

Under Fire, Ruth Brown Mystery Series, Book 1

Under Ground, Ruth Brown Mystery Series, Book 2

Under Cover, Ruth Brown Mystery Series, Book 3

Murder of Convenience, Women of Courage, Book 1

Non-Fiction

WWII Word Find, Volume 1

Linda Shenton Matchett writes about ordinary people who did extraordinary things in days gone by. She is a volunteer docent and archivist at the Wright Museum of WWII and a trustee for her local public library. Born in Baltimore, Maryland, a stone's throw from Fort McHenry, she has lived in historical places most of her life. Now located in central New Hampshire, Linda's favorite activities include exploring historic sites and immersing herself in the imaginary worlds created by other authors.

Website/blog: http://www.LindaShentonMatchett.com

Facebook: http://www.facebook.com/LindaShentonMatchettAuthor

Pinterest: http://www.pinterest.com/lindasmatchett

Amazon: https://www.amazon.com/Linda-Shenton-Matchett/e/B01DNB54S0

Goodreads: http://www.goodreads.com/author_linda_matchett

Bookbub: http://www.bookbub.com/authors/linda-shenton-matchett